BEAUTIFUL CONSEQUENCES

ANTWON RI'CHARD

Copyright © 2024 by Antwon Ri'Chard

All rights reserved.

Cover and interior design by Pat Maloney.

No part of this publication may be reproduced, distributed, or transmitted in any form or by any means, including photocopying, recording, or other electronic or mechanical methods, without the prior written permission of the publisher, except as permitted by U.S. copyright law.

The story, all names, characters, and incidents portrayed in this production are fictitious. No identification with actual persons (living or deceased), places, buildings, and products is intended or should be inferred.

First and foremost, all praise to The Most High for blessing me with the opportunity to create this body of work, which is intended to provoke thought and enjoyment in the readers who take the time to indulge. Hopefully, through my acts of service, I am able to redeem myself in your eyes. To my mother and my family, thank you all for praying for me and loving me even when my actions were not worthy of such. To Shaniqua Edwards, I appreciate your honesty about highlighting the things that are charming about myself and also connecting me with the next person I would like to acknowledge. To Crown Shepherd, I appreciate you being a call or a message away. To Lily at Beaver's Pond Press, thank you for not leaving me hanging. To Pat Maloney, the finishing touches would not be what they are, had it not been for your input. I'm thankful for you having been a part of this process and just as grateful that I was receptive to your suggestions.

*It's not always about the people you love,
but it's about the people who love you.*
—Random Wisdom

CHAPTER 1

It was still chilly outside. All I could see were the shadows from the trees we was passin', since the frost wanted to make a home on the window. This wasn't taking as long as I thought it would—we already had our layover in Chicago, and now this bus was taking us to Minnesota. I thought getting out of town was going to be more complicated than this, which is one of the main reasons I was hesitant to come out here in the first place. On top of that Bro talking about "he can't trust nobody out here." *Then why you want me to come out here, so we can't trust nobody together?* I thought. I was glad I didn't have nobody sitting next to me so I could lift the armrest up and stretch my legs out. Making this move had me feeling a mixture of nervous and excited. I had no idea what to expect coming out this way, but I was interested in seeing something new. *Detroit will always be there if I need or want to go back*, I thought. *Chances make champions, I can't be scared to make moves outside of my comfort zone. Hopefully Bro got things out here lined up the way he made it sound on the phone. Either way, ain't no turning back now.*

"Attention all passengers! This is your driver speaking. I just wanted to inform you that we are now arriving in downtown Minneapolis. Please make sure that you have all of your belongings, and check under your seat for any trash or anything that may have fallen on the floor during your trip. And once again, thank you for choosing Greyhound."

Damn! That was quick. I must have zoned out for a nice minute. Let me call Bro to see if he down here already.

"Hello," Marcus's voice came through the phone.

"What's going on, bro? I'm pulling into the bus station right now."

"Aight, bet. Just come to the front of the building. We out front waiting on you."

Getting off the bus, I could already tell Minnesota was a different world than Detroit. The bus station was not only bigger but also looked a lot more up to date. Walking through the bus station, things were calm—but as soon as I walked through the second set of doors, it was like something out of a *Grand Theft Auto* game. The bus station sat on a busy street in downtown Minneapolis. People were cursing, driving crazy, and honking their horns like they couldn't wait for the light to change or for the line to move. There were a lot of taxicabs lined up on the side of the building, I'm guessing for all the people traveling who didn't have cars and needed a ride. They had green-and-white, blue-and-white, and red-and-white cabs. I thought taxis were the same color everywhere: yellow. So I knew just from this new basic introduction that I was not prepared for this visit. Next thing I knew, I saw my brother walking toward me with some woman right next to him. This was the first time I met Pinky. It was kind of odd, since I'd never heard anything about her and then all of a sudden there was a physical being in front of me.

BEAUTIFUL CONSEQUENCES

She wasn't shy about anything and inserted herself into everything possible. The way I viewed it, it was like she wanted to show how important she was to what was going on. But that was exactly what I had come for: to see what was going on. We decided to go to Applebee's so we could eat and talk for a while. As we made small talk while waiting for our food, I started to think, *Why did Bro say on the phone he didn't have nobody he could trust out here but fail to mention anything about Pinky? Especially since they live together. I might be overthinking it, but why is she acting all needy and shit, like she's not confident in her position or something? She's trying way too hard. I don't know, maybe since I'm younger she wants to seem cool or something.*

After we ate, we hopped in a cab to go to their apartment. Once we got situated, Pinky decided to roll a swisher and put it in rotation. Marcus stepped out to make a sale. It was like she couldn't wait for him to leave, because as soon as he did she started to talk about everything.

"You know yo brother is out on three bails, right?"

"Three bails? Nah, he failed to let me know that on the phone."

"Well, I thought you should know. I went and got 'um the last time. This is the spot they just hit."

"As in the place we in right now?"

She just nodded her head while Marcus was walking in. She passed him the blunt, and I asked if I could speak with him in private.

"Man, why you didn't tell me all this shit before I got down here? We hot as hell sitting in this crib that just got hit a few weeks ago and wit you bein' out on three bails. I can almost guarantee the hook watching you."

"Bro, you trippin'. I got you. I'm about to move, my line slapping, and all we gotta do is move around."

As the days went by, I continued to see things that made me uncomfortable. My brother had allowed Pinky to be too involved in the activities surrounding his drug operation. He would literally go get the work, bring it back to the apartment, and allow her to break it down. That wasn't even the worst part: he let her serve some of his customers, and she even had her favorites. His phone would ring, and after the conversation she would ask who it was. Then after hearing certain names, she would be like, "I'll take care of dem," and the situation would be all in her hands. I understood that she was his girl, but it just seemed like sloppy work ethic. I didn't want to question him about it because I didn't know how deep their relationship was, but what was going on just didn't sit right with me.

"Bro, why you got Pinky breaking down and selling nah work? How you know you can trust her?"

"That's my girl. She good."

"Man, I don't trust her. But she's yo girl, so it's all on you."

One day in particular, they were arguing and the energy coming from Pinky rubbed me the wrong way. "So what am I supposed to do!" she said to Marcus. "You got all the money, all the dope, and all the fiends, so you think you just about to leave me with nothing?" This was definitely not what I had in mind when I decided to come this way.

Marcus's phone was doing numbers, but as fast as the

money came in, it was going right back out. They both had their habits, plus she wanted to smoke weed all day and night. She didn't work, so all the expenses were coming out of Marcus's drug money. And to top it off, their money management wasn't solid.

Then she would do slick shit. Like, if Marcus told her that they wasn't spending any money on weed, she would start an argument, go serve a customer, and take the money to go get some weed. Even though I was the youngest, Pinky was indeed the kid in this scenario and was more of a liability than an asset.

We decided that staying in this place was too much of a risk and moved to another location with a woman who Marcus sold dope to. Yet after a few days of us being there, as we were all out, Marcus got a call from this woman expressing how the police had just raided her house and showed her a picture of him, letting her know who they were looking for. At first, we all thought that she was lying, but when me and Pinky went back to the house and saw how it looked inside, we knew it was real. It looked like a tornado had hit. The insides of the drawers were dumped all over the kitchen floor, and the stove and refrigerator were on the opposite side of the room. The love seat and couch were flipped upside down in the front room, with all the contents from the cabinets all over the living room.

After we left the house that had just got hit, Pinky and I went to her sister's house for a while to chill while Marcus attempted to figure out where we were about to go next. After a couple hours, Pinky got a call from Marcus telling her to come pick him up, so we said our goodbyes and departed. As we were getting in the car, a tan Ford Taurus turned the block and started creeping at a slow pace. The two white occupants stared at us through their sunglasses and didn't take their eyes off us until their car passed ours. I knew at that point that we were being watched and it was time for me to go. As Pinky began to drive off, I sat in the passenger seat in deep thought. *I don't know who the fuck them white dudes was, but they was staring at us too hard. I wonder if this is coming from that raid that just happened yesterday. It could be, but then Marcus is out on three bails, plus the apartment was hit right before we came down here. Either way, it's way too much shit going on for me to sit around here like this. I'm gone.* When we pulled up to where Marcus was at, I was heated. I felt like things were spiraling out of control. It was like I was the only one who cared about what was happening—everyone else seemed unfazed. I got out of the van and it was like with every step my feet became heavier, like I could crack the cement if I wanted to. Once I got inside, I wasted no time expressing my thoughts.

"I feel like it's time to go. Now! Don't you see what's about to happen? How we relocate to another side of town and get raided dat quick. They showin' the house lady pictures of you, plus them two white cops I seen today scared the shit outta me. If I've ever seen a fed before, them was it."

"Lil bro, just chill. I'm getting this shit poppin', and I'ma move you and pass you da line."

"Bro, I don't think we got the type a time you think we

got. Everywhere we turn, the hook is right there. My mind is made up: I gotta go, at least until things cool down."

"If that's what you want, bro, I gotta let you make yo own decisions."

My bus ride back to Detroit left at 3 p.m., but I wouldn't make it home until the following morning. I started to gather the belongings I came with so I wouldn't be looking for anything last minute. I didn't come with a lot, only a few pairs of pants, a week's worth of underwear, a few T-shirts, two pairs of shoes, and my cell phone. On the way to the bus station, Marcus tried one last time to get me to stay, but nothing could convince me that staying here was a wise choice. We embraced before I left, and I made my way into the bus station. Fortunately, the bus wasn't crowded, and I had a row to myself. The bus ride back was unsettling. As I looked out of the window, my thoughts began to drift.

This was a total waste of time. Because of all the extra shit Bro had going on we couldn't even get no money like that. Then he had Pinky involved in everything. I don't know what was up with that. It would have been different if she wasn't moving all weird and causing extra problems for nothing. I don't see how he even allowed her to be a part of what he got going on, especially with all the risk involved. Then it was like everywhere we went the police was right on our ass, and that's just from what I was seeing. But he seemed like he wasn't fazed by it at all, it was either that or he was at the point that he didn't care. Or maybe he couldn't care. The most important thing is I got to invest time with my brother, nothing can outweigh that. Now I have to get focused and figure out what I'm about to do when I touch back down in the city. Hopefully Bro was right about me overreacting and things weren't as bad as they seemed, and I can just go back out there once things cool down.

I settled back in the city, and after a week I called Marcus's phone. Pinky answered and said, "They got 'um, they got yo brother. You was right, they was watching us the whole time."

I didn't know it at that time, but Pinky was in the car when Marcus got arrested. She snitched and told the cops that the dope in the car was his. We wouldn't see each other again for three years.

CHAPTER 2

That's crazy how I literally just missed getting jammed up out there in Minnesota wit bro. *I seen that shit coming, I don't know why he just wouldn't move around until things cooled down. Now I gotta figure out how I'm about to maneuver with the little money I do have. Once I get myself situated I can figure out how to reach him so we can stay in contact while he in there.*

After I made a couple phone calls, I was able to get myself into a spot to work in. The setup was smooth: all I had to do was wait until someone knocked at the window, ask them what they needed, and serve 'um. I just needed to be in the midst of some money flowing until I figured out what my next move was about to be.

I usually just sat in the spot and, if I needed anything, I'd just have someone make a run for me. But today I wanted to make a store run on my own. It was nice outside, so getting some fresh air didn't seem like a bad idea to me. As I was getting ready to step inside the gas station, I heard a voice yell out "Nephew!" Initially I didn't want to acknowledge the comment because if a person doesn't call me by my name, then I just don't assume that they're talking to me, but the voice sounded familiar. Once I looked up, I seen it was my cousin's dad.

"Unc, what's going on? I haven't seen you in a minute, what you doin' on knis side of town?"

"My ol' lady moved over here after I went in for a pistol the police found when they raided our crib. Once I got out, I shot over this way just to stay out the way for a minute so I could get my game plan together. What you got going on?"

"Nothin' much for real. I'm working in knis spot right now up under my peoples until I can figure out how to make a lane for myself."

"Well, my crib right around the corner from here, so if you ever want to come by or need somewhere to go, you're more than welcome."

"I appreciate that, I'ma most definitely come through and kick it with you and the rest of the fam. I'm about to head back to this spot. I'm about to call yo phone right now so you can lock my number in."

"I got you, Nephew, and be careful out here."

After the conversation with my uncle, I proceeded to go into the gas station to grab something to snack on. As I walked through the aisles and scanned over all the choices of candy, chips, cookies, and pop, I decided to grab me a 25-cent pack of split green apple and red cherry Now and Laters, a 50-cent red Faygo pop, a 25-cent bag of barbecue Better Made chips, and a $1 Slim Jim. After paying the cashier the two dollars for my stuff, I made my way back to the spot.

A couple weeks later, I got a call from my uncle. "Nephew, I'm getting ready to move back to the North End. If you want to, you could come wit me and we could make some shit happen together over there."

"That don't sound like a bad idea. What I got going on over here is cool, but I need a change of scenery."

I finished the last of the sack that was given to me and then made my exit on to my next adventure. The last time I was on the North End, I was a kid, so I didn't really remember too much about how the neighborhood was set up. There were way more abandoned houses over there than there were on the West Side, and you never really heard of anyone moving over here. Anyone that lived over there had already been there for years. Once I studied my surroundings, I was cool. I don't know what it was, but something told me to go get a job. I landed a job at Toys "R" Us and still sold weed on the side, which had me in a decent position.

As I was attempting to stay focused, my uncle—noticing that my attention was more on the grind than anything else—decided to give me some bad advice: "You gotta treat ya self, not cheat ya self, Nephew." From that point on, every time my uncle went and got fresh, I went and got fresh too.

As I was continuing with my day-to-day operations, I got a call from my older sister Brenda. "Little brother, what you doing?"

"I'm chillin', just working my job and tryna stay out of trouble. What's goin' on?"

"If you can, I need a hunnid to hold me over until I get my check."

"I got you, but you'll have to come get it from me. I'm on the North End now and I'm not mobile."

After she made the drive and saw me, the look on her face told me that she was uncomfortable with me being on this side of town. "What are you doin' over here?"

"I'm building wit my uncle right now, so this is where I'm at."

"I don't like you being over here. Just please be careful, and thank you."

I took my uncle's advice and started mismanaging my money. He had control of my bag while I was at work, so I was taking shorts on the weed I was selling. I went from having a consistent flow of income to basically having to push packs for my uncle to attempt to get back to where I'd been. I was hired at my job during the holiday season, and they wanted me to stay, but my hours would be cut until things picked up. I decided on the bus ride home from work that I wasn't going back. *At the end of the day, this shit is really my fault. I had no business wavering from my initial goal: to stack as much money as I could while living with Unc until I decided what my next move would be. Hopefully if I'm out on the block full time, I can rack up enough money to get me back on my feet.*

After a couple months of assisting my uncle moving the crack and heroin he was purchasing, I realized that the way he operated his business wasn't for me, especially since he wasn't paying me enough to match the work I was putting in. We had a conversation about our arrangement and couldn't agree to terms on how to proceed or what was owed to me, so I decided to pack all my things and head to the West Side to Brenda's house on West Warren.

"Little brother, what's going on?"

"Nothing, just tryna figure some things out. Where William at?"

"I just sent him to Minnesota with my older cousin."

Her son William was a few years younger than me. We all met a few years ago, once my dad got out of the Feds. Once my dad said *this is your family*, there was nothing else to talk about from that point. They all had my devoted loyalty. Whenever William had any issues with some dudes in the neighborhood, Brenda would call me, and I would come over with no hesitation to lay down the law for whoever wanted problems.

After I got the number from Brenda, I called William to see what he was on up there.

"What's goin' on, man?" he answered.

"Nothing really, just figuring out what my next move is about to be. When did you get up there?"

"A few months ago. You should come out here wit me. I could use you around. I don't got nobody I can trust, plus we gettin' some nice money dis way."

"I don't know, I just left from that way a few months back and shit was wild. But I do kind of need a change of scenery."

"That's why you should come up here. You can stack some money and we can kick it."

After the way the last situation in Minnesota ended up, part of me wanted to steer clear of that place altogether. But sitting around couldn't be any worse than what William and his older cousin had going on out there. I packed up what I thought I needed and headed back to Minnesota.

CHAPTER 3

"Welcome to my world, Unc!" William said to me as we entered the apartment. There were two guys sitting on separate couches in front of the TV. This was the first time I met Smooth, who later became one of my good friends. Now, even though Smooth was from the East Side of Detroit and I didn't rock wit dudes from the east, I didn't get a funny vibe about him, so we were good in my eyes. Then there was an older dude named City Boy. There was nothing really to say about him: he took care of business and did what needed to be done. That was it.

There was just one person missing that William was telling me about, and as soon as his name came up, he came walking through the door from serving a client. My relationship with Smack was basically over before it started. I knew that something was off about him, and I made a note to bring it to William's attention later.

We all ranged from age sixteen to nineteen, except for City Boy, who had to be in his late thirties or early forties. Everyone was in motion except for me. I just sat back and watched everything closely, rarely speaking unless I needed to, like always.

I still hadn't met the man responsible for paying for my ticket to come here. A few hours went by before Big came through the door with his chauffeur. He came in, dropped off a package, grabbed the money that was waiting for him, and then greeted me.

"What's up, lil cuzin. You came down here to get you some money, huh?"

"Yeah, man. Tryna get on my feet."

"Well, you came to the right place, Minnesota is nothing like Detroit. Plus, the way I got things set up, it shouldn't be too difficult to make things how you want them—as long as you stay focused. I got some more runs to make."

Big left and the adventure began. William was excited, of course. He wanted to show off a little bit and let me know how he had come up since he had been here. When I smoked weed before I came to Minnesota, I only really ever smoked reggies, because that's what was in my price range. The weed wasn't bad, but you did have to break down the buds sometimes in order to get the seeds out. Every now and then I would be able to buy some Ghan, but that was only on rare occasions. But when I got up here, it was a whole different type of smoke game they were playing. Any time anybody bought some weed, it was nothing but Hydro. You could smell it as soon as somebody stepped in the room with it, before they even opened the bag. It wasn't hard or crunchy when you broke it down, either—it had a nice, sticky texture to it, plus the bright green color with the red hairs in it reminded me of the ninja turtle Raphael. I was curious to know how the operation was set up, and just as the thought crossed my mind, William came through the door with a fresh package from Big.

"It's yo turn to break down the work."

"The work for who?"

"For all of us. Come to the back room." After he gave me the instructions on how to break down the package, he said, "I'ma roll up while you doing knat. After I'm done I'ma come back here and smoke wit you."

I sat at the table in the bedroom with a razor blade, a digital scale, and a box of baggies and broke down the brick of crack into eight balls. After I did a couple, Smack said out loud to everybody, "Man, his shit big as hell. The line about to be goin' even mo' crazy once we start sellin' these."

"Yeah, you right. How much you weighin' 'um at?" William said.

"You told me bag 'um at 3.0, and that's what the scale saying."

City Boy came into the room to see what we all were talking about. "Let's change the batteries and see if they still weigh up the same," he said.

As soon as we changed the batteries, the scale revealed that the work was overweight and I had to unbag the few eight balls I had already made. William asked me if I wanted to hit the blunt.

"Yeah, but my hands got dope all on 'um."

My fingers looked like they had just been dipped in a bowl of flour, so he held the blunt to my lips as I took a couple of hits and went back to what I was doing. At the end of the breakdown, there were about 2.5 grams of dope left, so I asked William what was I supposed to do with the leftovers.

"Whoever break da bag down gets what's left over, so that's all you."

For every package that Big dropped off, everybody got seven grams. In Minnesota you got ten dollars a tenth for dope, so for those seven grams you could make seven hundred dollars if you broke it down and didn't take shorts or sell eight balls. Compared to Detroit, where you'd be lucky to break down an eight ball and make $150, Minnesota was the land of milk and honey. Big had the operation banging hard. It was rarely ever slow, and we were going through the packages so fast that on most days one of us had to go meet him to re-up, sometimes two or three times a day. I started feeling like everyone was just living in the moment, going shopping and buying the best weed they could find right after they made their money off the package we'd just pushed. I had really needed to come back out here to learn my way around. From the time I had spent with Marcus, I knew what the money was like. But in order for me to truly dominate my position, I needed to move around and connect with people.

After a few months, I started to get irritated by how everybody was moving. They were getting lazy. At first, we didn't serve out of the apartment—we went out to meet people at a distant location—but then they started selling dope to people literally in the parking lot of our complex, which I knew put us all at risk of being exposed. Then, to make things even worse, they all just sat in this small-ass apartment with all this dope and no stash spot.

One day after my aggravation started to get the best of me, I questioned the group. "Why y'all just got all the dope out like dis in one spot. If they hit dis bitch, we all goin' Fed." They all just sat there looking at me like the idea had never crossed their minds. "All I'm saying is, this is too much dope to be right in here with all of us, plus all the money to go wit it."

Everybody just went on with their day as normal. After William, Smack, and City Boy had left, it was only me and Smooth handling business.

"Man, you right about what you said earlier. I mean we already taking risk, why make shit worse by not being careful?"

"I know, but everybody act like if Big don't tell 'um what to do, they can't think on they own. There's gotta be somewhere we can stash the work at in here where we can still have access to it." Me and Smooth went around the whole apartment brainstorming on how we could hide the dope. As you can imagine, we had limited options in a one-bedroom apartment, but I came up with something that I thought wouldn't be noticeable if we did get raided. It wasn't a guarantee, but it brought us some comfort to know that we had a chance.

A few months went by, and things weren't turning out the way I wanted. I didn't feel like I was getting enough exposure to the city to understand my surroundings. Then Big brought a few more guys from the city to the apartment, and to me things were getting overcrowded. Once I had made my decision to leave, I had a conversation with William. "I'm about to get ready to go back to the city, Nephew. Not only is shit overcrowded, but they serving people too close to where we lay at. This ain't no dope spot!

If that was the case then we would just serve straight out dis bitch."

"I feel you, but leave and go back to what? You might as well stay here until we figure shit out."

I don't know what it was, but I felt this urge to move around. I had heard the stories of the raids that they were in before I got here. In one raid, the police found an ounce of crack in Smack's boot, but since he was still a minor at the time, they paid for him to fly back to Detroit and never come back to Minnesota again. But of course he came back. I needed to work through my thoughts, and I wouldn't be able to do that in the midst of everything going on.

"I gotta go, but I'll be back. That's on everythang."

"Alright, Unc, just be safe and stay in contact."

A few weeks after I left, the same spot I was in got raided. They found over fifty thousand dollars cash in the raid, but as crazy as it sounds, the police couldn't find the dope for nothing. The police assaulted William, thinking he was flushing the dope in the bathroom. But after they realized he was a minor, the guys were all taken to jail and then let go. A few years later I got close to one of the other guys that was also caught in that raid. I found out that the DEA did come to interview that one person, and no telling who else. Yet no one was charged for the money that was found. And as far as the dope, the crew was able to go back to get the nine ounces that was stashed in the apartment after they got released.

CHAPTER 4

I was only in Detroit for a few months before William sent word that the crew in Minnesota wanted me to come back. There really wasn't much to think about: the money was a lot better, and I liked making moves out of state instead of sitting in the city. Once I got back, I noticed everybody was moving around a lot more than the last time I was out here. Now this was more to my liking—the movement helped me develop a better sense of the area we lived in. I also was able to gain a few personal clients outside of what we were doing for Big. William and Smack started bringing the girls they were entertaining to the house we were living at. That was the first time I met Gabrielle, a girl that William was dating at the time.

As fate would have it, the ones around me started getting sloppy again. They started bringing people too close to the house out of laziness, plus Smack's girl came over to the house and put open condoms all over the fence in the front yard. We lived in a duplex, so you can imagine the complaints from the neighbors. Then, out of the blue, William got pulled over in a rental we shared. He said the cops mentioned that they had been watching us. Next thing you know, a cop car was sitting on the block a few houses down from the house, and I could see 'um right from our window.

"Man, I know y'all see dis shit. Nobody else doing nothing on knis block but us, but how they know where we living at?"

"I don't know, but this shit is crazy. What should we do now?" Smooth said.

William called Big to see what he thought. "Man, he said for us to stay here and not to go nowhere, that we tripping," William said.

"What? Man, look, I'm about to leave for a little while, fuck what he talkin' about."

Then we all hopped in a cab and went to the Mall of America for a few hours. When Big called us, nobody wanted to answer, so I picked up the phone.

"Why is nobody here? I told everybody to stay at the house. You little dudes need to come back."

"Look, I already told you the situation. I'm not about to sit in that hot-ass house when they blatantly watching that bitch. We'll be back when we get there."

"So y'all just do what y'all want and not what I say, huh? All I'm saying is when I was up under the man I was working for and he said 'stay here no matter what,' that's what we did. Fuck the police, a blizzard, hurricane, or whatever."

Time went on, and we eventually relocated again. Same side of town, just a different area. I ended up getting Marcus's information and figured out how to get in contact with him while he was still in prison. He connected me with his new girl, Brittany. From the first day we met, she embraced me like her brother, and once she got her house, she gave me automatic access. Gabrielle introduced me to her older cousin Porsha, and since I wasn't entertaining any females at the time, I was open to us getting to know each other. After a few conversations, we decided to go to a popular spot called Pizza Lucé for our first date. I didn't have a vehicle, but Brittany let me take one of her cars so I could pick up Porsha. I didn't know my way around Minneapolis that well, but Brittany told me how to get to Porsha's house, which wasn't that far from where she lived. Once I pulled up, I called her to let her know I was outside.

"Hey, did you have a hard time finding the place?"

"Actually, it was kind of easy. Ey, do you got yo license? I don't wanna be driving around here, and I don't got no L's."

"Yeah, I got my driver's license."

"Ok, well why don't you drive so we'll be cool if we get pulled over."

She drove to downtown Minneapolis to Pizza Lucé. It wasn't crowded, so we grabbed a booth by the window, ordered some wings, and made small talk. For a first date, things went smooth, like we didn't have a dull moment during the whole date. I found out that she was a dental assistant and in the process of moving into her own place. After we ate, we sat in the car, smoked a blunt, and then ended our date. We hung out a few more times after that, but nothing happened. Gabrielle and William had just had their son David, but things were always a hassle. She and William fought and argued a lot, to the point that William just didn't care for her. William confronted me about still having contact with Gabrielle, but he couldn't deter me from being real with her.

"Whatever disagreements you have wit her is between y'all. She ain't never did nothing wrong to me for me turn my back on her, so why should I just up and stop talking to her?"

"Man, fuck her. Leave that bitch alone. She a dirty bitch."

"Man, you need to quit doing her like dat. This her first kid and it's yo third, she gon' need yo help. Whatever the case, just because you mad at her don't mean I'ma stop talking to her."

"Whatever, man."

As the months went by and David got bigger, I would go check on him and Gabrielle. I met Gabrielle's older brother a few times when I went over, and he embraced me as family.

One morning, Porsha hit me up and wanted me to come over to her place, so I slid over to see what she was on. We were just chilling in her apartment, but then the next thing you know, I was looking at the tattoo of her name on her lower back as I was making her ass clap. Neither of us ever talked about being exclusive with each other, so what happened wasn't anything major, nor was what was between us worth any further searching.

Things were a bit rocky for me the next couple of months, but nothing could prepare me for the road I would have to travel down next.

CHAPTER 5

I hadn't seen my brother in three years, and it was finally time for him to be released. Brittany was going to drive to Moose Lake to get him the morning he got out, so I stayed the night at her house the night before. I'd never been locked up before, at least not for a long period of time. I couldn't imagine having to be in a place like that for as long as Marcus was. I was laying on the couch when Brittany walked in and I saw Marcus's frame towering behind her. Our dad was 6'2", and Marcus was a few inches taller than him, but I didn't inherit the height from that side of the family since I was only 5'8".

"Lil Brooo," he said as he reached out to slap my hand, and then we hugged each other tight.

"Damn, Bro, it's been a long time. Don't look like you lost much weight since you been gone."

"Nah, it ain't too much to do in there but work out and eat. I was mostly eating." We both started crying laughing.

"I was waiting on you so I could roll up."

"You can go ahead, Bro. I'm not smoking until I touch a hundred thousand."

"That's a huge goal."

"Not really, you'll see."

It took Bro a few months to get adjusted, but once he figured out how he was about to move, it was on. We strategized on how we could collaborate and corner the market, but then all of a sudden Brittany started to act different. They began to argue a lot, and it was starting to remind me of how him and Pinky's relationship was before he went away. They were really just starting to be around each other for the first time, and I had to fall back and let them sort out their issues.

Not even ninety days after being released, Marcus and Brittany were about to get married. That morning, after we got dressed in our suits but before we left to head to the church, I pulled Marcus aside. "Look, Bro," I said. "Marriage is no joke. I understand she was there for you when no one else was while you did yo time, and I commend her for that. She was there even when I couldn't support you. I see you both got the matching tattoos and all, but this is a different lane. Don't do dis shit if you don't feel it."

"I know, man."

That was all he said, but from the look in his eyes, I knew that he didn't want to walk down that aisle. Regardless, it was his decision to make, so I supported him without judgment. The holidays were approaching, so we were doing what we could to stack as much money as we could. During the holiday season, people spent all kinds of money just for the sake of keeping traditions going. These crucial months could either put you in the hole or keep you stagnant for a while. I had just come back from Detroit for Thanksgiving with the family, and then me and Marcus had a disagreement about our business arrangement. I felt it was time for me to move around anyway. He and Brittany had too much going on for me, plus it was time for me to stand on my own. I was more than capable at this point and had another place to stay, so I moved my belongings from Minneapolis to St. Paul and continued handling business solo.

Even after the disagreement, if I needed something that I knew Marcus had, I made sure to keep the money in the family and spent it with him. One time when I went to pick up something from my brother, he had his friend Chris over. Chris had known Marcus for ten years, and he was from Detroit too. When I first started coming to Minneapolis, Chris introduced me to a few people who turned out to be solid clients, but besides that and us smoking a few blunts sometimes, that was where shit ended. That night, an argument broke out between my brother and Chris. My brother wanted to smash Chris, but I initially tried to resolve the situation by telling Marcus to chill. Then things spiraled out of control, and me and Chris had words, to the point that Chris implied that I was dick-riding him when we first met. In my mind, I was like, *The nerve of this clown*. Even with me having no clientele when I came back to Minnesota, I know I probably came with more product than this weirdo had seen in the last five years, and I was ten years younger. I just was never the dick-riding type, it just wasn't my character, especially toward a bum of such low stature. Chris was a washed has-been—well, really a "never-been." He was just one of those types that know the people who get money, never really the type to be making no big moves on his own. He was finished and I knew it, but I was getting tired of arguing with him, so me and my brother kicked him out the spot and things settled down for a minute. Then my brother got a phone call and jumped up like he levitated himself off the ground and said, "Where you at?" As he ran out the door, without me thinking about the move I was making (which was an out-of-body experience for me), I ran right behind him and jumped in the car. It was complete silence on the way to Chris's house, and it seemed as though all the lights were green on the way. When we got in front of the building, my brother called Chris and told him to come downstairs so they could box. But he wasn't trying to come outside, and with each passing moment the anger in the car rose. Still, with all the trash-talking he was doing, he wasn't about no action. Suddenly two shots were let off in the air and we rode off. But that wasn't the end of the situation.

CHAPTER 6

The next day things were calm, and we didn't talk about what happened the night before. Word had spread amongst the D-Boys, and the ones on the outside of the direct situation were trying to settle things so it wouldn't get ugly. On top of everything else, Chris didn't live alone—he stayed with another guy from Detroit named Michael, and he was furious about the shots being let off in front of his building. He was telling a select few people that he was coming to see Marcus and me about what happened.

That night, me and Marcus was at the house chilling in the basement. I was playing a game on my phone when Marcus's phone rang. He didn't get to the phone in time but realized after it stopped ringing that it was Chris. We ignored it, but not even twenty minutes later it rang again, same caller, so he answered.

"Where you at?"

"I'm at home. What's up?"

"We about to slide through dhere." *Click*, he hung up the phone. Once they arrived, they exited their van and approached the house. Me and Marcus met them in the front yard. Chris walked past me and I paid him no mind because I knew Marcus could take control of the situation from behind me. My attention was on Michael, and his attention was on me. Even though I hadn't heard about Michael being a threat per se, I considered him more of a concern then the man who just walked past me. Once Michael got close enough, he asked me something regarding the shots being let off in front of his building, and as I was about to respond, all my sensors went off at the same time and a strong urge told me to turn around. As I started to turn around, I was struck in the temple with a hard object that felt like iron. I'd been in plenty of fights, but I'd never felt anything like this before. The hit sent a shockwave through my whole body that left me in a numb state. Not only could I not feel anything, but it was like I blacked out and for these few vital seconds I couldn't see anything at all. I was in sheer darkness and numbness, all my senses told me that I was in severe danger if I didn't act. It was like it all happened simultaneously in separate motions that coincided together. I was struck with the object, I blacked out, the numbness took over my body, all of my senses was screaming I was in grave danger, and all of a sudden *boom, boom, boom, boom, boom, boom,* a barrage of shots were fired. I came back after damn near being knocked unconscious, but the man who was once in front of me was no longer there—he was laying on the ground in the driveway. I thought, *How'd he get down there?* As soon as the thought went through my brain waves, I realized that my gun was in my hand. The shots I heard came from me. I instantly turned around to find my brother beating the shit out of Chris, dropping his ass with haymakers and, as soon as Chris fell, picking him back up to drop his ass again. Someone else who was at my brother's house called out to me, "Man, get the fuck outta here. Run, man, go." At first I was stuck. It was like I was in a trance. But after the individual shouted out to me again, I snapped back and took off running. As I took off through the backyard a woman screamed, and then I heard, "Get on the ground, get on the ground!" I continued running, but I knew that the police were really close, so I decided to jump in a hole behind a house to hide for a while. Somehow, I made it to the spot where the initial altercation took place. William buzzed me in, and as I came up the stairs toward the apartment I was in a panic.

"We gotta go."

"What you mean, what's up?"

"Shit got ugly, and we gotta leave here now!"

I didn't want to talk about what happened since there were two other people there, so we called a cab. As we waited, I couldn't think straight, but I knew that we needed to get off this side of town. We weren't too far from where the shooting happened, and I knew that with certain people knowing about this location I could be caught by the police before I could figure shit out. I should have gotten a few numbers out of my phone, powered it off, got rid of it, and taken the phone of a woman who was there to network off of and returned it later, but my mind was too clouded. The cab got there and we left. William called Big's brother, and he pulled up on us—then we jumped out of the cab and hopped in the car with him. Nothing was said in the car, but once we reached our destination, I explained what happened. Big's brother instructed me to cut my phone off and not power it back on again, but before I did that, I called Brittany. The event happened right in front of the house and even though she was gone at the time, her children were in the house, so I called her to see what she knew.

"Hello?"

"Where you at?"

"I'm at the house. Bro, the police is everywhere. You okay?"

"Is the police right in front of you?"

"Yeah."

"What about Michael?"

"Bro, he dead."

"For real?"

"Yeah, and Chris was saying yo name to the police before I could even get into the house, saying you shot Michael."

"Aight, I'm gone."

"Make sure you cut yo phone off." *Click.*

"Fuck!"

Big's brother and William looked up at me. "What?"

"Michael died, and on top of dat Brittany said that Chris already told the police that it was me who shot 'um." I started to cough up blood as black as a nightstick. I think the combination of being assaulted, then hearing that Michael died, plus knowing that my name was given to the police as the shooter, all was a lot for me at one time. My face started to swell at an enormous rate, so I put some ice in a bag and held it on the spot to attempt to reduce the swelling. With me not being of a darker hue, it looked like I had a plum on my face.

Someone called Big, and he offered me some sound advice, since he had been through this type of situation before. He told me to get as much money as I could and leave town until I could get properly prepared. I felt trapped just sitting still, but I didn't know how to move in this situation. I couldn't settle my mind. Big's brother was about to leave and asked me if I wanted a ride. I should've left, but for some reason I stayed. As me and William sat at this location, Bob, a drug user we both had known for a while, dropped by. He was initially there to meet someone else, but since they weren't there he started growing impatient. "Hey, do one of you guys have something?" he asked.

With so many thoughts racing through my mind, all I knew was that I needed as much money as possible so I could lay low until I could come up with a strategy. Moving recklessly, I activated my phone and called the woman at whose place I had stored some of my belongings. We drove over there, and I got out of the car and went into the building. Once inside, I went straight to my stash, but before I could get to it, she said, "Oh my god, what happened to you?"

"Nothin', I'm cool."

"Whoever did that to you need to be dead."

I grabbed what I came for and headed back to the truck waiting outside. There was a big snowstorm expected to hit that very night, and it was coming down hard. As I approached the truck, I had a weird feeling in my stomach. There was a car with its headlights on behind the truck, but I figured it could have been someone else in the building, so I thought. If I had been thinking clearly, I would have noticed that the car was way too close to the truck. Once I got close enough, two officers jumped out of the truck with their guns aimed at me and ready, yelling, "Don't move!" They apprehended me and threw me into the vehicle that was behind Bob's truck.

Little did I know, I was being tracked off my phone, and with the information the police had, the dynamic of my life was about to change forever.

CHAPTER 7

Beep... Beep... Beep...
I struggled to open my eyes. Everything was blurry, and it took a minute for things to become clear. *Where am I?* I thought. My eyes went from the ceiling to the door. Then I glanced at my feet. "Man, what the f—"

Before I could get the last word out, I saw a strange man at my feet. I attempted to jump up, but my arm was handcuffed to the edge of a bed.

A woman's voice came from my left. "It's okay, you're going to be alright. Just do your best to calm down." She put her hands on my chest and shoulder.

Once my mind settled, I realized that I was in the hospital. The strange man at the foot of my bed was a corrections officer. Everything started to come back to me play by play.

Once I arrived downtown to the Hennepin County jail, I was rejected due to my injuries and had to be seen at the hospital before being booked. The X-rays revealed that I had a fractured orbital socket bone and cheekbone and was scheduled for surgery two weeks later. The booking process was pretty much a blur for me—all I really remember is getting a green wristband put on that had a picture of me on it with my name, height, and weight. Then I was put in a cell by myself with just a steel toilet, a desk, and a mat on top of a concrete block, which I think they considered a bed. I sat in that cell for a few days, not really knowing what was going on. Every morning for breakfast they would bring something called a "cutie pie," which basically was a dessert and a milk. I wasn't hungry or couldn't eat, so I just gave it to the person in the next cell over from me. One morning, after they had brought breakfast around, some papers were slid under the door to my cell. They were charge papers. The writing on it seemed like something from a foreign country, but eventually I realized that I had been charged with second-degree murder. I would be lying if I said that I never thought that I would possibly end up in jail for one thing or the other, but never for a charge like this.

Before an officer escorted me to general population, I had to switch into the county jumpsuit and give them all my belongings. I literally had to give the underwear I had on.

They handed me a brown T-shirt, some brown boxers, an orange jumpsuit, a pair of orange socks, and some brown slippers. As I began to put on my new uniform, I started to wonder, *How did I switch my pair of white Lo's for an orange jumpsuit?*

After I got to the unit, the deputy told me what cell I was in, and then I was left on my own to figure out anything and everything. My bail hearing was the next week, so I had to learn how I was going to operate in there until I figured out how this was going to play out. That morning before my hearing, they called out the names of the people who had court right after breakfast. They handcuffed us hand-to-hand and feet-to-feet while we walked from the jail to the courthouse. After we all were uncuffed, we sat in the bullpen. When my name was called, I stood up to the podium. The judge read off my charges and set my bail for a million dollars. After hearing my charges and how high my bail was, thoughts of never getting out of jail started to flood my mind. I wanted to cry, but as my eyes started to water, I shook it off. Even if I wanted to show some type of emotion, this wasn't the place for that.

As soon as I got back to the unit, I heard my name over the intercom. I wasn't expecting a visit from anyone, but when I got to the window, it was Porsha behind the glass. I hadn't called her since being arrested, so I knew the only way she knew what was happening was from Gabrielle.

"Hey," she said.

"What's goin' on? What you doin' down here?"

"I heard what happened and I wanted to come see you. How you doin'?"

"I'm alright. Just waitin' to see how things gone play out."

"I want you to know that I love you, and when I get my income tax money, I'ma take a few thousand and put it towards your lawyer."

I was taken aback. This definitely wasn't the time to be feeding into people's emotions, which were probably just based off my current situation. I didn't want to sign up for a line of support that I knew she couldn't follow through on. But I wanted to see if she was just talking when it came to the lawyer money though.

"I don't expect any support in this situation. I just have to work through it."

"Five minutes," the deputy said as he walked by our glass cubicle.

"I'll make sure to come see you at least once a week. This isn't far from where I live."

"If you can come, I appreciate it. And if not, then that's cool too. Why don't you show me what them titties look like before you leave."

After we hung up both phones, she lifted her shirt and held up both of her breasts for me. There was no telling when I was going to be able to see a naked woman again, so I had to get what I could out of the situation. We talked a few more times after that visit, but once she got to acting funny I had to cut it short.

Throughout the months that I sat in the county going back and forth to court, Gabrielle came to visit me often. She came to see me once a week at least, sometimes more than that, plus we talked on the phone a lot about everything—how the case was unfolding, how she and David was doing, what was going on between her and William, and what females I was entertaining at the time. She was extremely supportive, even to the point that throughout my time in the county she racked up a three-hundred-dollar phone bill from accepting collect calls when I couldn't put money on the phone. A few weeks before I was scheduled for trial, the state offered me a plea for twelve and a half years. In the state of Minnesota, you did two-thirds of your time in prison, so I would do eight years behind a wall and the rest on parole if I took the deal. This was a critical decision for me: I understood what had happened, and in no way was I attempting to not be held accountable for my actions, but I genuinely had been acting in self-defense. I also still had to be mindful that this was a murder charge, regardless of how I felt.

After weighing the pros and cons of going to trail, I reluctantly took the plea. Before I was sent to prison, Gabrielle came to see me. The conversation in that visit was hard, but she lightened things up for me. "You could have got twenty-five years. Now with what you took you still stay in single digits. It could have been worse."

"I know."

There was a brief silence as my thoughts started to wander. I was twenty-two at the time I got my charge and would possibly be thirty once I got out. In my mind, thirty was old-man status. I figured I would have gray hair and wrinkled skin.

"This is crazy," Gabrielle said. "But me and you are so close, and we get along so well. What if it was me and you together instead of you and Porsha or me and William?"

Now this was something that had never crossed my mind, not once. I cared about Gabrielle but never looked at her in that type of light before. Plus she had a child with William. But I knew she was right. "I know, we would be so good together."

Things got silent at that moment as we looked at each other, the way we viewed each other slightly changed, but we both knew that we were entertaining something that we shouldn't, so we ventured away from the topic. That would be the first time the topic of us being together came up, but it surely would not be the last.

CHAPTER 8

"Reid, time to go."

It was 5:30 in the morning the day I was being transported to prison. I was already awake, since I couldn't sleep the night before. Before you leave the county jail, they have you sign over all your belongings to someone to come down and pick them up. All of my family that I could trust to do something like this was out of state, so I just put down Gabrielle's name. That ride to prison was uncomfortable to say the least. Having my hands and ankles cuffed together reminded me of when I had to be transported to the hospital to have surgery on my face. I remembered how people looked at me as I walked through the hospital cuffed, with my orange jumpsuit on, with a corrections officer with me. I had heard stories about prison, and they were never good. It was always some crazy, scary shit happening, so I was on high alert.

When I arrived, they gave me a week's worth of socks, underwear, and white T-shirts. I got two blue button-up shirts and two pairs of jeans, along with two free envelopes. A CO escorted me to the front desk so that I could figure out what cell I was going to be in.

"You're going to be in cell 36, galley C," the receptionist said.

The CO had me follow him up the stairs to the galley I

was on and told me to walk straight down the block until I got to cell 36. I could hear all type of shit being yelled from the cells as I walked in.

"Fresh fish."

"New meat on the block."

Once I was there, he slid the lock open. I got inside, and then he locked it back. I had the cell to myself, which I was grateful for, but there were two bunks in this cell so I knew at any given time I could get a roommate. At county, I had a door that locked me in, but this was actually a cell with bars, and I could hear everything that was going on around me. I turned on the light at my desk and started to write two short letters to use the two free envelopes I had. One was for my mom and the other was for Gabrielle. As I was writing, someone walked by my cell and said, "You want cleaning supplies so you can clean your cell?"

"Yeah, I appreciate it."

He gave me a cleaning solution that he told me was for the toilet, a spray bottle for me to use to spray down the bunk and the closet, a broom and dustpan, and a toilet brush. Then as he handed me a stack of paper towels.

"I'll be back with a bucket of clean water so you can mop if you want."

As I was cleaning my new area, I just couldn't wrap my mind around how I was going to do so much time. I had just turned twenty-three a month ago.

It was hard to get into a routine. In my initial days, I found myself just calling people, wasting money talking to them out of necessity, trying to remain out in the free world. I needed to figure out how to stay in control of this situation and not let it control me. Then I made a conscious decision to stop using the phone completely—anyone outside my immediate circle wouldn't hear from me, even some I considered family wouldn't hear from me either. I didn't want people sending me money, because I wanted to figure things out on my own and learn how to maintain things in here.

For the first couple months, I was lost. I really didn't know what to do with myself. Then I got moved to a different unit with one of the older homies from Detroit named B. Me and him were in the county together and ended up getting the same amount of time, since B had an attempted murder case. We kicked it every day—once he figured out who my peoples was from back home, we was locked in. Then another guy named Bird came to the unit. Once Bird found out who I was connected to, he considered me family from that day forward. I wasn't one to trust people too fast, so I decided to accept the alliance but watch my surroundings heavily.

Bird had done Fed time before and tried to get me to work out with him. "Come on, relative, you need to start exercising."

I kind of ignored him and started to zone out again. He came to sit next to me.

"Look, you gotta take care of yoself in here, relative. Nobody is gon' do it fa you."

Then he went into a mini speech about the benefits of exercise and how it kept your stress levels down. Next thing you know, it was me and him getting it in. In the beginning, I felt embarrassed. I couldn't even do one pull-up and needed Bird's assistance. The wristband I had on in the county jail said I weighed under 140 pounds, so for me to not even be able to do one pull-up on my own, I was weak as fuck. I watched certain dudes hit the whole rack, twenty plates, on the bench press. I thought that these guys must be the strongest dudes in the world to be able to do that—I couldn't even budge the rack.

"Always remember when doing knis, do what ya body can do."

CHAPTER 9

After working out consistently for a few months and taking whatever educational courses the prison would allow me to take, I finally got into a routine. I really just stayed to myself. I didn't gang bang, so that eliminated a lot of problems for me. Outside of some guys from Detroit and a select few people I'd done business with on the outside, I didn't know any of these dudes, so I felt I shouldn't have any problems. I stopped focusing on the outside world so much and put my attention on how to establish a foundation and rebuild so once I was released, I would be on my way to greatness.

As time went by, I started to understand what people meant when they said "out of sight, out of mind." I didn't hear from anyone unless I reached out to them. It was odd to me that I was stuck in one place but I had to reach out to those who I thought valued the relationship we had. But I also had to remind myself that just because I went away didn't mean life had stopped for everyone else out there. The one person who I could not apply that analogy to was Gabrielle—it was like she never allowed my situation to come in between us, and I loved her for that. Gabrielle was a constant in my life. No matter the situation, if she brought it to my attention, I would always give her the most prudent advice I could offer her.

Even when we lost contact for a while, I didn't hold it against her. She still wrote me, and we still talked on the phone, but just not as much. Whenever I did talk to William, I would always ask where she was, how she was doing, and about David's well-being. She'd had another child, Aaliyah, and that was partly to explain for her absence.

One day I was in my cell, and thoughts of Gabrielle surfaced. I remembered one time when we were on the phone before we lost contact. I'd heard a voice in the background say, "Girl, who is you on the phone wit? You haven't stopped smiling since and it's like you not even here."

"My baby daddy," she said. "And don't worry about what I got going on."

I told her not to play like that. Even though I knew I shouldn't have liked what she said, I did. Gabrielle was special to me, but as I felt I was putting too much energy into the thought, I shook it off.

CHAPTER 10

After two and a half years, it was time for me to be transported to a medium-custody facility. When you arrive to prison, they evaluate your custody level due to your case and previous offenses. I started out as level 4, but as these couple of years went by and I didn't get into any trouble, my points dropped and now I was at level 3.

As I was transported to the new prison, a feeling of uncertainty traveled with me. The new prison was set up totally different from where I'd just come from. It was more like a college campus than a prison. There were no more bars on the cells—these were actual rooms, and they actually had bathrooms, not just toilets in the room you slept in. When I got to the unit, there were a lot of people in motion, and I stood reading the signs attempting to figure out how things were run over here. As I was reading, I saw a close friend of mine named Steve walking down the hallway. He was just coming back from work and only had a short period of time before he had to be back.

"Man, it's good to see you. I'm glad you ended up over here and not at one of those other medium facilities. This the place to be when it comes to level 3. I'ma put in a good word for you so you can get in at the job I'm working at, and you'll be able to put you some money up while you're here. I'll be going home in a little over a year, but that'll be enough time to get you in position to where you'll be all the way good when I leave."

After I got my work schedule together, I was able to create my workout routine and balance the rest of my day-to-day activities. I was really into reading business and personal growth books like *The 48 Laws of Power*, *Rich Dad Poor Dad*, and *The Secret*. I didn't really like reading urban fiction books, even though I did like the "Blood of My Brother" and "The Cartel" series.

After a brief conversation with William, he gave me Gabrielle's new number. I was excited to talk to her and eager to hear what had been going on in her life. When I called her, she brought me up to speed on everything, her new daughter, how David was doing, where she worked, and how she was doing personally. We were back talking on a consistent basis, and even though I didn't do my time on the phone, I talked to her whenever I had the chance.

"Where all those females that was writing you and you had me three-way calling?"

Once I left the county, she had gone downtown to get my property and seen all the letters I had from women who wrote me.

"You know how it is. Everybody love you until you get that time, then you're on your own."

"I know, because there's not a single one of them around now. I was there for you so much that you tried to make me your woman."

"I have never tried to make you my woman."

"Yeah, you did, Brandon, I can't believe you denyin' it."

BEAUTIFUL CONSEQUENCES

"Gabrielle, you don't think I would remember comin' onto you like that?"

"Well, something is wrong wit yo memory, because I remember it."

"If I wanted you to be my woman, you would be my woman. So if I did come onto you like that then what happened?"

"I don't know."

"Exactly. So let's just move on from this subject. But I never came onto you like that."

"Let's agree to disagree. And yes, you did. You wanted me to be yo woman, it's okay." She laughed.

CHAPTER 11

Me and Gabrielle were reunited, and it seemed that our connection was stronger than ever. One day when we were on the phone she was riding with her sister and a few friends.

"I got somebody who wanna talk to you."

"Talk to me, talk to me about what? Who you talkin—"

"What's up, how you doin'?"

"I'm alright. Who is this?"

"This Ashley, do you remember me?"

I did remember her, but only vaguely. I couldn't picture her. She was Porsha's friend back when I used to talk to her. I remembered picking them up in a rental I had and letting Porsha drive with Ashley riding shotgun while I chilled in the back. She used to kick it with William's cousin back then.

"Yeah, I remember you. You're Porsha's friend, right?"

"Not anymore, but yeah, that's me. So what's up wit you?"

"I don't got too much going on, just knocking this time down."

"How much time you got left?"

"A little over two years."

"Oh that's not bad. Take my number down so you can call me later."

I told her that I would and to tell Gabrielle that I would get at her another time. I wasn't the type to just jump into something blindly, so I wanted to check with Gabrielle about why Ashley decided she wanted to talk to me all of a sudden. I hated wasting time, and I was more focused on having teammates than having a committed relationship. I wanted to have someone I could count on, in comparison to just talking to somebody to pass the time by. But I was always open to building with someone who could be a potential asset.

"Ashley's cool. She be out here doing her thang, moving around a lot. I mean all I can say is she's an adult entertainer."

If Gabrielle said she was cool, then I just left it at that. But in the back of my mind, I wondered if Gabrielle indulged in the same activities as Ashley, since they were so cool. After a few phone calls, Ashley did seem like she could be a loyal woman when she wanted to. She even took a dope case for a guy that was on parole, but he left her in jail, didn't bail her out, didn't get her a lawyer or anything. I kept those traits about her in the back of my mind because I knew people like her just needed the right person around them to reach their potential. Other than that, I really didn't see anything else between us, partly because my mind started drifting towards someone else.

Gabrielle.

CHAPTER 12

*D*amn, *what am I supposed to do now?* I knew I could talk to Gabrielle about anything, but this was different. *Should I say something?* I valued what we had: it was a real genuine bond, and this could potentially bring friction between us. We had always been close—it was like nothing could come in between us and we could always count on each other. Even though the concept of us being together had been brought up a few times, I never pondered it long enough to create an actual life of its own. What if she never looked at me in that type of way seriously? What if this turned us against each other? Not to mention the other people that surrounded us.

I cared about her so much that if I did decide to tell her how I felt and she didn't feel the same, I could accept it. We could still remain great friends without any hard feelings. I trusted her like no one else, and I had always told myself that once I got out, I would always be there for her no matter what or no matter who liked it. I tried to push her out of my mind a few times, like I had done before when thoughts of us together would manifest, but this time it was different. I didn't want to cross that line, but my mind kept drifting to her, and my emotions started to take over. I wanted her and no one else. But how? The past was the past. I slept with her cousin once before I came to prison, and she had a son with William. I was stuck and couldn't figure out what to do with the level of comfort between us.

I decided to call her. I would never forget that day—it's when everything changed. She was on her way home from work with the kids in the back seat.

"How was your day?" I asked.

"It was okay. Nothing really bad happened."

I paused for a minute to gather my thoughts.

"You know I really love you, right? Like as far as you being here for me and everything, I'ma always be there for you no matter what when I get oudda here."

"I love you too. I know you are, I don't worry about that," she said in a sincere voice.

"I want to tell you something, but I don't know if I should or if it's the right time yet. I'ma write everything down, and then I'll get back to you, okay?"

"Alright, I love you."

"I love you too."

I was a hopeless romantic at heart, but no one really knew that. Expressing myself passionately was something I could do with no effort. Once my heart was involved, there were no limits as to what I would do to show my love. I always loved to write, an asset I developed during the days when I desperately wanted to become a music artist. Now I needed to let what was in my head cover the pages of blank paper.

After a few days, I had a twelve-page letter expressing how I felt to Gabrielle. It was deep, passionate, and full of energy. There was a lot of power and love in those twelve

pages. I was even surprised at the things I was saying, but love does that to you.
I called and Gabrielle answered the phone. "Hey."
"I finished writing down everything."
"How long was it?"
"It's a lot."
"For real, how long is it?"
"Twelve pages."
"Damn, that is a lot."
I was still hesitant. I cared about Gabrielle a lot and didn't want to complicate things between us by revealing how I felt. After things were silent for a moment, I said, "I'm still confused about what to do, so I'ma ask you. Do you want me to send this to you now or wait until a later time?"
"You can send it to me now. I want to know what you're thinking."
"Are you sure?"
"Yes, send it."
"Okay, have a good day. I'll talk to you later."
"Okay, I love you."
"I love you too."
I went back to the two-man room that I was in at the time to think. It had literally taken me days to compose what came out on those pages—then I had to rewrite it to format it properly so that it would sound right and the delivery was heartfelt. After I reread the final draft, I sat back thinking.
I had never looked at Gabrielle like this before, and I felt I was crossing the line. She was William's son's mom,

and I wasn't supposed to be entertaining emotions like this when it came to her. Even though me and William were not close anymore, he still considered me family, and this could be looked at as a sign of betrayal in his eyes. Then I thought, *How am I crossing the line? They're not together. They have a child together, that's it. If I love her, then that's what it is. I can't help who I love. They'll just have to respect and accept it.* Even with all the obstacles, I couldn't shake the fact that I was falling for her. I knew if Gabrielle and I were to be together, some people wouldn't agree and would criticize or ridicule us. But once they realized that we had something real, it would blow over.

As I looked back through the years, when people would say they loved me, it would make my stomach turn. I knew it was fake and they didn't mean it. Their actions never matched their words. But with her it never felt artificial. It was "out of sight, out of mind" when I came to prison, she just didn't fit that mantra. She never let my coming to prison come between our relationship—that's why I cared about her so much and would always be loyal to her.

I needed to know where she stood, and we could figure everything else out later. Before I mailed the letter, I sat in the room with it in my hands. I knew this could change everything between us. If she didn't have these types of feelings for me, I could accept it and leave it alone. But if she did, we had a lot to discuss. This could bring us closer together or drive us farther apart. I prayed over the envelope before I dropped the envelope in the box. There was so much power in those pages that once the letter was gone, I felt a lot of energy leave me. All I could do was wait for her response.

CHAPTER 13

Aww that means a lot I swear it do I got the letter I'm kind of lost at this moment I don't know how I feel but I will say I do want you to know me better. I'm here for you always and that's real of you to feel that way and let me know you want to see me win instead of taking away from me like most guys do. I respect you so much and I love you that's all that matters I don't know what we can grow to be I don't think it can be on a serious level because of how we know each other it just won't be right. I hurt William enough I don't want to hurt him again I'm here that's all that matters. I've been busy not ignoring you, anyways I have to go pick the kids up now love you talk to you soon here's a pic of me for you though.

After reading Gabrielle's email, the uncertainty that had been lingering in my thoughts was replaced with a mixture of rejection and sadness. But I knew she was right. I knew it would be a lot for us to be together, and even if William and Porsha weren't really hurt by our relationship, they still could play the part in order to get people to judge us.

This is where most people would turn away and leave the situation alone, but not me. For some reason I felt that we could really be something. I just didn't know what. It had been a few weeks since we spoke, and I was thinking about doing something nice for her for Valentine's Day. I emailed her and asked her if she liked flowers, and if it would it be alright if I got her some for the special day. I figured I would get her a dozen roses and a fruit basket from Edible Arrangements. I would do a lot more if I was out, but I figured that should be sufficient enough to get my point across. I got the address to her job and set up the delivery for the gifts. It was two weeks before Valentine's Day and everything was alright, but as we were talking on the phone Gabrielle said that her car was acting weird, and once she got it looked at, the mechanic said she needed new tires.

"How much do new tires cost?"

"Shit, like six hundred dollars. But I could get some used ones from anywhere between two and four hundred dollars."

"Do you got the money?"

"No."

Now even though I was in prison, I wasn't hurting for nothing financially. It wasn't like I was rich, but I had a few thousand in my account and, recognizing how fortunate I was, I didn't penitentiary ball. I had a budget and stacked as much as I could—why ball hard in jail only to come home looking for handouts? It just didn't make sense to me. I bought the necessities and that was it.

This wasn't a place to sit back and get comfortable. This was a critical time to self-reflect and correct errors within myself. I had strong feelings for Gabrielle, but the thought of sending money out of prison never crossed my mind until now. I had once read a passage in a book that said, "Whoever you give your money to is who you give your power to," and I was a firm believer in that. Me and Gabrielle had prior conversations where she expressed that she didn't get the help she needed from David's and Aaliyah's fathers and how she felt she had to handle everything on her own. I felt her pain—it was like whatever affected her affected me. I had told her that I would always be there for her and vowed to her that she never had to feel alone as long as I was breathing, that she would always have me no matter what. Another woman couldn't get anything out of me, but the connection between us was different. I loved her and wanted the best for her and couldn't just sit back and do nothing if I had the means to help, so I sent her three hundred dollars.

After I did it, I couldn't believe it. I didn't even know what to think, so I left it alone. I just wanted to support her and be there for her.

OMG so I just checked the mail out of the blue & it's a check for $300 from you I'm so lost for words, that's a lot of money you giving me when you're behind bars love. I'm thankful but I feel wrong for taking it, it's yours you need it more than me I work everyday. Idk I'm thankful but that's a lot I don't want you doing that anymore. I love you I wish I could send it back or some that's too much. I can't take from you I don't feel right. Call me in the morning, I'ma make sure to answer Love you

As the months went by, our connection got stronger. We didn't talk every day, but it seemed like we did. I wanted to know everything about her. She was my best friend, plus I loved her and, above all else, I trusted her. She expressed to me that she had worked as an exotic dancer before but nothing past that point. I didn't judge her, but I hated that, even though she wasn't my woman, a part of me felt like she was. I didn't want any other man touching her, let alone seeing her exposed body, but I knew I had to accept it. I would just support her regardless of what she did because I cared about her that much.

I knew that things with us would not always be sweet because of all the elements involved. One day we were on the phone and I could feel the tension between us, so I asked her about it. "What's wrong wit you?"

"What do you mean?"

"You know what I mean, it's like you don't wanna talk to me or something."

"If I didn't wanna talk I wouldn't have picked up."

"What's the attitude about? Did I do something to you that I don't know about? I can call you another time."

"If that's what you wanna do."

"What, you don't fuck with me or somethin'?"

"It's not like you my man!" She said it with such force that it kind of threw me off.

"I'm a just give you some space. I'll talk to you later."

"Alright."

This was the first time we really got into it, but I knew it was a lot to deal with. Us trying to be together came with a lot, and she probably felt that the potential drama would be too much, even if she did love me. I gave her some space for a few weeks and then I called.

"Hey," she answered.

"How you doin'?"

"I'm okay, what about you?"

"I don't have a choice but to be okay."

"I hate when you say that."

BEAUTIFUL CONSEQUENCES

I felt like she was avoiding me, not answering my calls or responding to my emails, so I had to say something. "Is this how it's gon' be between us?"

"What do you mean?"

"You dodgin' me now?"

"It's not like that."

"Then what's it like then? I know you see me callin' and what, you too busy to respond to an email now?"

In the most innocent and purest voice I had ever heard from her, she said, "Baby, I have to treat you like this so you won't like me anymore."

"You don't have to treat me like this. I love you, Gabrielle. Our situation is complicated, but the love between us is real. We can figure this out, my feelings are not gon' change."

"Okay, baby."

"I love you, and I'll talk to you later."

"I love you too."

CHAPTER 14

Good Morning!!
Hmmm, I haven't heard your voice in days and to be honest I don't like that, I miss talking to you. Do I ever think maybe we will be something when you get out? Hmm idk I don't try to think about it, do I think we wouldn't be on this page if you weren't in jail? I can't say that because we were so close, maybe we would of or maybe not. I don't try to think about us being together because I know it's not right. I have grown to really care and love you and maybe not in the way I am supposed to. I just don't want to lead you on and I'm not ready for what us may come with, what I will say is that I know you love me and it feels good to have someone love me for everything about me. It feels good to have you in my corner, you're so far yet so close. Can you send me a form so I can come visit you, is it far from the city? I really want to see you face to face, I don't want to wait until you get out. I wonder will you feel the same seeing me. Anyways I'm not doing much I'll probably go to a bar later on and have a drink, I have so much on my plate I need to find a job asap! I'm a little jealous you talk to someone else on a daily, I didn't want to tell you I was but I can't be mad because I'm not around to talk to you daily and I talk to people so I have to be fair. As much as it might not be right to say, I don't want nobody to take my spot. Idk I'm thinking too much right now and you know I hate opening

up, here are some pics of me let me know if you get all three of them. The newest pic is the one with the robe on that's from last weekend, so is the one with the long hair, the one with the bun is a few months back. Write back asap! I love you I love you I love you I do! Hope I put a smile on your face and didn't leave you too confused. Your love is so real and your loyalty is everything, don't ever change being that way, you have a heart worth more than money can buy, I really appreciate you I don't tell you that enough. I know you're thinking what got into me today huh lol but TTYL.

This was the first time she had completely opened up to me about how she felt. It was usually me expressing myself to her, but her message not only gave me clarification about her true feelings toward me but also uplifted my spirits. I couldn't stop smiling. She had me in a whole other world. With my emotions at an all-time high, I still wasn't ignoring the fact that she did entertain other guys. I didn't like it, but I had to accept it for now. I decided at that moment that I would only make time for her, to let her know that her spot could never be taken and was secure for life in my eyes. I went as far as cutting off all the other females I was talking to so I could focus on building with her.

As me and Gabrielle continued to build our relationship, I was also taking college courses. I wanted to obtain as many credits as I could while I was in so if I decided to go to college once I got released, I would have a nice amount of credits under my belt. I was in an English comp class, and the instructor always had us writing essays, but I couldn't really get into it because I wasn't passionate or en-

BEAUTIFUL CONSEQUENCES

lightened about the topics given. Anybody could fabricate some bullshit about anything, and that's exactly what I was doing. In a one-on-one meeting, my instructor, Ms. Short, pointed out her concerns.

"Brandon, I just don't feel like you're putting your best foot forward. It's like you're doing the bare minimum, and I know there's more to you than that."

"I feel I do what you ask of me. I don't know what else you want from me. It's hard for me to write about things that I'm not passionate about."

I knew what Ms. Short wanted—she wanted me to shed some skin and open up.

"You have to write something to grasp the reader. You want them to be taken into the world you're writing about."

"I'll try to do better."

"There's more to you than what you're portraying. I know that."

Later, a classmate of mine was reading an essay he had written on strength. "It takes strength to overcome your fears and go after what you want in life. It takes strength to be who you truly are in this world. It takes strength to stand up for what you believe in, even when no one else is standing with you. Without strength—"

I sat in my desk, my mind drifting to thoughts about me and Gabrielle's relationship. *Am I trippin'? Do I really love her, or is this some prison love shit?*

But I knew this wasn't any bullshit. I really loved her and wanted to be with her. Even though it would be viewed as wrong by certain people, I wanted to go about it the right way. I wanted to talk to Gabrielle's mom and family, to get their perspective and see how they felt, even though my feelings would never change. I wanted to express to them how I felt about everything, even the past. I wanted to disclose how much I loved Gabrielle and really had thoughts of asking her mom if she would give me her blessing to marry her. Then I would have separate talks with William and his mom. I know at first William would be totally against it, but I wanted to make sure that just because me and Gabrielle decided to be together, he didn't think he could stop being in David's life. William's mom at first wouldn't believe me, but once she looked in my eyes, she would know I was serious. They could not consider me family anymore for this, and I understood what could happen, but the love I had for Gabrielle overpowered everything else in my eyes. I was willing to deal with the ridicule and criticism for our love.

Idk what to say about your message, I couldn't believe what I was reading. You're so closed off when it comes to the subject of us, I'm so happy you opened up a little. I know the connection we have kind of scares you but it's undeniable, we love each other. We both are jealous when someone else comes along and has interest in either of us, we want our spots to be secure without the risk of loss. Let's be real, you don't want to share me and I don't want to share you, we want it to be just "us" with no other outside influence. I accept you talking to other dudes now because I know I can't provide for you like I need and want to but once I'm home I would like that to change. What's crazy is that even with me being gone almost eight years when I touchdown, I know that if you tell me yes for us being together, that

BEAUTIFUL CONSEQUENCES

you're all the woman I would ever need. I wouldn't want to be with anyone else, I can honestly be dedicated, devoted and loyal to only you. Before I got your message I was thinking the same thing, like damn I miss her and want to hear her voice. I think you know that I have what you've been looking for and I plan on giving you all the passion, energy and love I have inside me so you can fully understand that I adore you. You've never had a man cherish you like I do and will once I come home, that treats you like you're the most beautiful woman on earth because in my eyes you are. That's going to appreciate you to the fullest and not take you for granted, who's going to take pride in putting a smile on your face because it will bring me joy to know that I can make you happy. I want to be all the man you would ever need, I want to be able to stimulate you in all elements mentally, physically, emotionally and yes even sexually as well. I've never wanted to eat no woman's pussy as bad as I do yours, I crave you baby. I hope your pussy and my dick is a perfect fit. I want to see the look on your face when I'm stroking you from behind, while smacking your ass and pulling your hair all while I'm saying "I love you Gabrielle" Or you riding on top of me and we look at each other and smile, then I lean up and suck on your nipples as your pussy gets wetter and wetter. It's something in particular that I want to do to you but I won't tell you, you'll have to wait until I get home to find out. With all this being said I wish you would stop fighting me and just let this be what it is. You know you want to be with me so let's make this happen the best way we can. Either way, no matter if you acknowledge "us" now or not, the clock is ticking and your husband is coming home for you.

    I love you baby.

CHAPTER 15

I had another essay to write for my English comp class, but this time I had my choice of topic. For a while, I couldn't come up with anything, but my mind drifted to my relationship with Gabrielle. I titled it "Love" and expressed how I appreciated our bond and how she affected me. On the last day of class, everyone had to share one essay they wrote during the semester, and when it came time for me to share an essay, my teacher asked me to share the one that was inspired by Gabrielle. After I read it, my teacher and a classmate of mine suggested that I share it with the person who inspired the writing. I had never thought about sharing the essay with Gabrielle or anybody—I was just going to dispose of it—but the idea was tempting. I wondered if she would like it.

"I feel like I keep surrounding myself with all the wrong people," Gabrielle told me over the phone. "I'm starting to feel stuck. I know I get easily distracted and the people who are supposed to support me seem to do things that keep me away from going in the right direction."

"If you know all this, then you have to do what's best for you, even if that means separating yourself from certain people in order to accomplish your goals. It doesn't mean that you don't care for those people anymore, it just means that you're taking the things you need to do more serious.

If they can't respect you and where you are, then you don't need them in your life right now. If it's meant, then they will come around, and if not, then they have served their purpose in your life."

After I got off the phone with Gabrielle, I went to grab my blue coat and orange hat and signed out to go to the courtyard so I could walk around and do some laps and think. I would do one lap around the courtyard, and once I made it back to the exercise equipment, I would do a set of pull-ups and push-ups, then continue with my walk. Listening to her tell me about the people in her life opened my eyes more to how things could be for me once I got released if I didn't stand firm on my goals. Energy is infectious, and allowing the wrong people around you damages your progress. We all at some point of time fall victim to allowing people to be in our lives longer than they should be, which costs us for not cutting ties sooner.

"Yard closes in ten minutes. Yard closes in ten minutes."

As I finished my final lap before I went back in, I started thinking hard, *What can I do to help her?*

CHAPTER 16

I knew that, since I wasn't out there to be on Gabrielle's ass about handling business, I needed to find another way to reach her. I was always reading personal growth and business books and had a lot of quotes and material written down that I could share with her. I found thirteen cards with motivational sayings that I could send to her. I decided that once a week for the next three months I would send her a motivational card with a few quotes from my notes. I knew I couldn't be there in person, but I tried my best to be there for her mentally and emotionally.

One day she told me one of her friends had promised her some money to get David a hoverboard, but her friend never came through, and she didn't have any other extra money to her name and was struggling bad. I hated to hear her like that, desperate, hurt, and stressed. Her pain was my pain.

I told her not to stress and that I would send her five hundred dollars. If I was out, there would be nothing that she would have to go without. I would make sure to contribute to all her bills and David's and Aaliyah's growth. I always stressed to Gabrielle that she was never alone as long as I was breathing.

She told me she wanted to go to school to get a degree, but I could sense her hesitation. I encouraged her to enroll in college and just take a few classes at a time so she wouldn't get overwhelmed. She also had two interviews for jobs coming up, so she was excited. When she started her English comp class, she was a bit intimidated, so we worked together on two of her homework assignments. One day she emailed me about an argument she had with William where she brought up my name. Willam told her that I was a chump and that he made sure I ate. She sent me the text messages of them going back and forth, but I really didn't feel any type of way about what he said. I never talked down on William to anybody at all—I just wasn't dealing with people like I used to. I was focused on me and Gabrielle building our connection, so to me it didn't matter.

At this point I was closing out my sixth year of being in prison, and if I could stay out of trouble I could be out in a year and a half. My mind got to racing, but I had to settle it because even though that seemed like a short period of time, it was all about staying focused and clear of distractions. One day, when I called Gabrielle, she was getting ready to go dance. I hadn't heard from her recently and missed her, and she could sense my energy.

"What's wrong, baby?"

"I don't know, I'm probably thinking too much."

"About what?"

"Us."

"I want you to understand something: you're in there and I'm out here. I don't want you stressing about me or us. You know I love you, Brandon, right?"

"Yes, I know, Gabrielle."

"We both know what it is. I tell you everything. You don't have to worry about nothing. When you come home, we're going to see where this takes us, but until then let's continue to support each other until we can be together."

"Okay, baby." She knew how to calm me down. Only her words could comfort me no matter what I went through.

"I have to finish getting ready. Now tell me, 'Go get some money, hoe.'"

"I'm not saying no shit like that to you."

"Say it, baby. Tell me."

I reluctantly obliged. "Go make some money, hoe."

She laughed. "I love you, baby."

"Be careful, and I love you too."

I didn't like that she danced, but I loved the fact that she didn't hide anything from me. Saying that made me feel like I was encouraging her to shake her ass for other men, and I hated that. A few days later, I wrote her an email stating that even though we weren't together, she was my woman and that's what it was. A few days after I sent that email, we were having a great conversation and the energy was intense, so I figured it was time for her to tell me something that I wanted to hear.

"Tell me."

"Tell you what?"

"That you my bitch."

"You crazy."

"You made me tell you 'go make some money, hoe.' So tell me."

She paused like she was zoning everything out, and in

the sexiest voice, she moaned, "I'm yo bitch. Ugh, I'm yo bitch, Brandon. I'm yo bitch, baby."

All I could say was, "Damn, for real?"

She laughed. "See, that's why I didn't wanna do it."

"Don't trip. I'm not gone off you yet."

"We'll see how long that last."

I knew I was in love with Gabrielle because I wasn't holding anything back. I cared about things with her that had never crossed my mind with any other woman, like her sexual history—I just wanted to know so we would be able to make memories only for us to share. I wondered about her father. She never spoke about him, and I never remembered him being around even before I came in. Gabrielle made me jealous, nervous, and insecure sometimes, and no other woman has ever been able to make me feel those emotions. I didn't want no other man to be able to touch her. I knew I just had to keep it together until I got home. It was my birthday, and I was feeling good even though I was locked up. I had just turned twenty-eight and knew I would be home soon. I hadn't talked to Gabrielle in a while, so I made it my business for us to talk on my special day.

"Gabrielle, what's today?"

"I don't know, tell me what today is."

"You really don't know?"

"No, I don't. So tell me."

"It's my birthday."

She gasped like she was trying to catch her breath. "Oh my god! Happy birthday, baby. Aww, happy birthday."

Then, in a sexy voice, she asked, "Is yo dick hard while you talking to me?"

"You know it is, baby. Can't no bitch get my dick hard like you can."

It was like my dick rocketed up instantly just from her asking about it. Luckily, I was using one of the corner phones. But even with me sitting down, I had to adjust myself and put more of my white T-shirt over my gray sweatpants.

"Damn baby, how much time we got left?"

"We under two years now."

"Don't play with me. For real, under two years. I can't wait until you get home, baby."

"I can't wait until I come home either. You know I'm coming for you, right?"

She got quiet, probably thinking just how fast time would fly by and I would be out and we could be back in each other's lives.

"I just wanted to hear your voice today. You made my week—fuck it, you made my month today talking to you. I miss you, baby."

"Aww. I miss you too, baby."

"Be good and be careful out there. I hope the kids are good, and I'll talk to you later."

I was gone off Gabrielle. She had me wrapped around her finger and I knew it. I was whipped and would do anything to make her happy and put a smile on her face. One day, we were talking and she was telling me about how she went on a date with some other dude, but she didn't like him and he wasn't her type.

"So you entertainin' other dudes and going out on dates now?"

"At least I told you. Don't be mad."

"I'm not. I don't like it, but I'm not mad."

I loved how open we both were with each other. We told each other everything, so nobody could tell me anything about her that I didn't already know. She knew honesty meant everything to me. There was no reason for us to come this far only to start lying to each other.

"Plus, I've been thinkin'. I don't feel like I need a man right now. I'm feelin' like I should just work on myself and just have you."

"Wait, what you say?"

"You heard me."

I couldn't believe my ears, it was like my prayers had been answered. "It's up to you. You already know I'ma always be here."

We were talking more often than before, and our connection was getting stronger. She expressed to me that she wanted to know more about me. She felt we always talked about her, so she wanted to know more about the man I was. This was around Christmastime, and I was attempting to figure out what I could do special for her. Since she wanted to know more about me, I decided to send her two essays I wrote in my English class—the one she inspired, and one I wrote about myself. I hoped she liked them. I valued her perspective and opinion more than anybody's.

CHAPTER 17

ood Morning Babe,
Waiting on you to call me lol I'm sure you will soon but not soon enough so I'm writing you. I was talking to Ashley a little about you and IDK she understands my feelings about it and feels like why not focus on me and wait for you to get out. I love her for understanding this situation, it's just a lot so I only share little things with her not everything. I love you and that's just what it is I accept the fact of that, just so hard to see how I'm going to handle it. I think you should start on writing a book, just try it out and see if it's something you enjoy. I can't wait for you to get out and for us to really enjoy life with the kids. I can't believe I've been around most of your whole bid s/o to me lol I never pictured this being a place we would be or even mean to each other. I love the man you are growing to be, I remember when you used to sound so sad and down. I love that no matter what you are, you stand by who you are!!! I'm trying to work on me, it won't be easy but I'm ready to find myself. Anyways I'm about to take a nap before I go get David and Aaliyah. Love you Brandon
XOXO
Wifey

It brought joy to my heart knowing that I wasn't the only one who could visualize a future for us. The new year came, and I knew if I could stay smooth then I would be released next year sometime. I did everything to stay focused on getting out and building with Gabrielle. I did speak to one other woman sometimes, but she would always question me about me and Gabrielle's relationship because, when she initially asked if I consistently talked to anyone else, I told her the truth. I wouldn't let anyone come in between me and Gabrielle. I could care less who didn't like our connection.

"Don't ever let anotha bitch question you about me. I'm not worried about her for I know you love me. She needs to fall in line."

"Don't worry, I checked her. She knows her place and nobody has the top spot but you."

After that conversation I felt like she was acting funny, like she wanted to push me away or she was trying to get me to treat her like I didn't care about her. But that would compromise my core values and feelings for her.

I probably just need to fall back from the situation, I thought. *I'm putting everything I have into this, but at the same time she doesn't even know what she wants or if she's ready to be with me or not. I'ma just send her an email and let her know my perspective.*

After I expressed my thoughts to her, she sent an email back.

I have to be quick and write this for I have to be at work at 3 and it's 2:22pm anyways I have really thought about everything you said and I want to tell you that I do want to give us a try and your love is more than enough for me and that no man out in these streets can show me half the love you do from behind bars. I love you and I'm ready to see what this can be and I'm sorry for treating you less than you deserve. I spent my last money on some stamps so we can write each other since you won't have phone time like that. Hope to hear back from you I'll give you some time. I love you baby I do. I'm scared I'm nervous to start this journey but the love you show me I know with God we can't do nothing but grow stronger and closer. It won't be easy you have to hold my hand and teach me I promise to be the best learner. Anyways I have to go before I be late.

Even though my heart was full of joy after reading her message, I was still reluctant to give in all the way. I loved Gabrielle more than I could have ever imagined possible, but I didn't want to be hurt by her. If we were to be together while I was in prison and she cheated on me, that would kill me. With me not being there physically, I knew that my spot was always at risk. No matter how much I loved her, I still always felt that the distance could harm us. I sent her another email.

I just came from outside, I just walked around by myself to clear my mind and get some air. What am I going to do with you? Lol a relationship, marriage, kids I want it all but only with you. I don't see it with anybody else, I don't want it with anyone else, you're it I feel it and nothing can convince me otherwise. This year cannot end fast enough, I need to be home with you. I see it: Us living together, a two-income household with you not having the burden of all the bills, us helping the kids with their homework, us cooking together (me smacking you on yo ass while you're telling me to taste this to see if the food is good or not). Us at David's games to be supportive and encouraging, us assisting Aaliyah with whatever her heart pushes her to do (cheerleading, ballet, dancing, you know girl stuff or whatever she wants). Family vacations, us taking memorable trips alone to places people rarely ever go to or get to see. Do you know how happy I'm going to be when you tell me you're pregnant? I can't even imagine the emotions I'm a feel because right now I feel such joy and excitement just thinking about it. Us laying together at night in each other's arms, being able to kiss those lips goodnight (both pair). Being able to go to sleep and wake up to your pretty face every night and morning. Me finally putting a ring on your finger and you in tears as I do it, as you say the words that might even bring tears to my eyes: "Brandon yes! I'll marry you." I want this with you Gabrielle I want this so bad you got me gone. Sometimes I don't even know where I'm at. Just when I think we can't go further it gets deeper, my love for you continues to grow by the day, my emotions set new limits and then I figure out it's limitless. Now I know what unconditional means, it never ends, it's in constant flow and rotation but only going higher and deeper, not remaining stuck in one spot or at one level. I told you my life would not be complete without you. I want you by my side baby, I'm waiting for you I promise I won't hurt you, come home baby where you belong. If you really do feel like I'm missing something or lacking in any area, Baby just teach me how to love you the way you want to be loved and I'll practice, I'll get better and be perfect at loving you. I don't want you with anyone else, I want you with me, but you have to want me just as much as I do you. I'll teach you and you teach me, communication is what's going to get us where we need to be. Look how strong we are right now, we can't stand being away from each other, it's a punishment for us not being together.

Even when we live together and we have our careers going,

we'll get a little time apart but we won't want to be away from each other too long. Look at how much love, passion and emotion is between us, just think about how it's going to be when I come home next year, we won't be able to stay away from each other. No matter what I'll never be happy with you being with another man. Even if you were to say let's wait until I come home for us to be together and you told me you were dating some dude or fucking some other guy, I would always have an attitude and problem with that, you know that. I want you to be fully committed and loyal to me, no half ass bullshit because I'm giving you my all so I want the same in return, is that too much to ask?

CHAPTER 18

'll get to a few things that have been bothering me today, I seen Porsha last night and she asked about you. She had this big grin like she still had a thing for you then she asked when you were getting out and suggested we should go see you. I played it cool but deep down it bothered me so much, it makes me question even going through with anything. I love you but I want to wait until you get out to see what happens with us. I think it's best we wait I don't want to think about the discomfort we may cause people by us being selfish to other's feelings. I just want you to remain being my best friend and we shall see how things go once you're home. I don't want to hurt you or me or my loved ones by my choices and as of now I'm just confused. I'm tired of being overwhelmed by this it's time to put the thought of us on hold and just focus on being here for me please. Anyways I miss you I really hope you understand me and don't try to push my decision or change how I'm feeling. This has been on my mind so much so that's what I've decided. I hope this doesn't hurt you I hope you really get me and know this is from my heart. The love I have for you will never fade and no one can stop that but things need to just wait. Smile, I'll always be by your side, I'm not leaving your side.

    What do she mean she wants to wait? I thought. *I don't have time for her to be allowing how someone else feels to dictate how we conduct our relationship. I'm tired of other people having an impact on what we got going on. She needs to really figure out what she wants to do because I'm at the point where it's all or nothing with me.* Our next conversation wasn't the best, and I knew it was headed in a bad direction.

"The circumstances are what they are," I said. "If we wait or be together now, what's the difference?"

"I said I want to wait. Respect my decision, Brandon."

"I am."

"So why do you keep pushing on it? Leave it alone."

"Why do you think? I get out next year, so to me, whether we have a title or not, we're still working towards the same outcome."

"I don't want to wait for you."

"What?" I had to pause to look at the phone like I didn't just hear what I knew I heard.

"I said I don't want to wait for you, Brandon. I like somebody else."

"You don't want to wait for me, and you like somebody else?"

"That's what I said, and if you can't call me on some cool shit and just check on the kids, then we probably need to stop talking."

I couldn't believe what I was hearing. "What do you mean just stop talkin'? Why are you talkin' to me like dat?"

"We need to just let this go. If you need time to get over me, then I'll give you some time."

Devastation gripped my heart. I heard what she said, but it wasn't registering correctly in my brain.

"Time to get over you, what the fuck do you mean? Gabrielle, are you listening to yoself?"

"If you don't get it, my actions will show you what I mean."

"So what, you just about to shit on me now? How did you go from wanting to be with me one day and the next you like somebody else? That don't make no sense to me. Gabrielle, I love you, you know you my heart and I'm not complete without you. Baby, it don't have to be like this."

"It has to."

"No it don't. I love you too much for it to be like this."

"Brandon, please leave me alone." I could hear the tears.

"I love you, Gabrielle, and you know I won't leave you alone."

"Brandon, you have to. Please."

"No." Silence. "Hello . . . Hello . . ." *I know she just didn't hang up the phone on me,* I thought. *What the fuck is wrong wit her.*

I called again and listened to the automated message. "Hello, you have a prepaid call from . . . Brandon . . . an inmate at a correctional facility. To accept this call, dial zero." *Beep.* "This call is from a correctional facility and is being recorded and monitored. Thank you for using GTL."

"Did you hang up the phone on me?"

Between sobs she said, "Yeah . . . I just can't do this with you right now."

"Gabrielle."

"I can't." She hung up again.

She had never spoken to me like that before. *This is really not making any sense to me right now,* I thought. *We might have had our disagreements before where things got a little heated, but the tone in her voice today was cold and vicious and I don't know who that person is.* The whole her-liking-somebody-else thing bothered me to my core, plus she actually hung up the phone on me—complete disrespect. *I don't know what to do or what to say, but we are going to have to figure this shit out if we're going to move forward in any type of way.*

Days passed, and she didn't answer my calls or respond to my emails. Then days turned into weeks, and I came to the realization that she had actually cut me off.

CHAPTER 19

As the months passed by without hearing from her, I started to get more and more frustrated and my mood started to turn. I continued to work out, but my mental condition just wasn't balanced. Life wasn't the same. My thoughts were becoming so heavy that it seemed that the room I occupied couldn't contain the energy that was vibrating from my mind.

I don't know what's up with me. My workouts haven't felt the same lately. Let me get on this scale real quick to see if I'm thinking too or if I need to pay more attention to what's going on.

The scaled beeped. *I'm down 20 pounds? How? I haven't been doing any excessive running. My appetite has been off, but I just don't be feeling like eating like I normally do. Nothing has been in the normal fashion lately, my attention span and concentration have been nonexistent. Elevating my mental capacity has always been a top priority, but I've been too weak lately to get a grip on the situation.* Besides my mom, no woman in the world meant as much to me as Gabrielle did. Yet with all my efforts, she had left me hanging, and that was so hard for me to believe. At times it was like I wasn't even in the present moment, wondering if my love for her was destined to break me, but why? My mind was controlling me instead of the other way around. I couldn't understand what was happening, but being distraught like this was crippling me to my core.

Over the intercom, I heard, "Reid, number 356256, come to the front desk. Reid, number 356256, come to the front desk."

As I made my way to the desk, I saw two red boxes at the counter.

"How you doing tonight, Mr. Reid?"

"I'm cool, what's going on?"

"You're getting packed up tonight. Those boxes are for you."

"Damn." Due to overcrowding in the prison system, they were randomly sending people to different county jails throughout the state to stay for up to a year. At county, you were locked into a cell or room and couldn't move around like in prison. On top of that, your selection of food was smaller and more expensive. This was a total inconvenience, but I had to do my best to adjust to this since I had no control over what was happening.

Luckily, I was transferred to a unit with a pull-up bar. Plus the jail gave us phones, so we could text any number for nine cents a text. Once I got my hands on mine, I let my mom know what county I was in and then I sat back.

It's crazy how I haven't spoken to Gabrielle in like four months, I thought. *Maybe I should message her to let her know where I am in case she tries to reach me and can't figure out where I am. Nah, I gotta quit catering to her. If she wanted to keep in contact then she wouldn't have allowed this much time to go by without hearing from me. I've always tried to be understanding when it came to her, but it just seemed like it was so easy for her to cut me off.*

I gave in to my emotions and messaged her, and as I was texting her what I had to say I realized that I was going to have to send two messages. After I sent the first, she responded, *Who is this?* Then once I sent the second text, she asked why was I in the county. After that we didn't talk for a few days.

She really sat back for months and watched me call her phone and didn't answer, not once, like she had a new number or something, I thought. *I'm not about to just let go that easy.*

I called and asked her, "How can I love you with all my heart and you hate me with all of yours?"

"I don't hate you," she said.

"Then why are things like this between us?"

"I'm with someone now, and I want you to respect that."

I hated the fact that she was putting another man over me. I felt that I should be the top man in her life, which caused us to start arguing once again.

"Why do you keep shitting on me? I'm always there for you. What did I do to you?"

"Brandon, it's just too much. You love me too much."

"You're the same person who said you loved me for the way I love you, and now it's too much? What am I supposed to do without you? I love you, Gabrielle."

"Brandon, I don't love you like that. Around the time you get out I'll have a baby and everything. You need to let this go."

At that moment, my heart broke. My emotions took completely over. "Gabrielle, are you serious? A fucking baby? I accepted you being with someone, but you're going too far. What about the baby we talked about? You just about to have this dude's baby like that? So just fuck me, right?"

"Brandon, I'm sorry. But it just is what it is, and you need to get over it."

I couldn't stomach the things she was saying. I felt humiliated. "Was any of it real?"

"Yes, it was. But I just can't. I shouldn't have let you fall for me when I knew I was unsure about my feelings. Sorry."

At that point I just left her alone. I couldn't believe how she had no regard for my emotions and how she was treating me. I was hurt bad. I would never have treated her that way or thrown something in her face, especially a relationship with another woman. She was doing me dirty. I sent her one last message.

"Was this your plan the whole time? What, you wanted to break me? Well, you have, Gabrielle. You have broken me to tears. I've never felt this way about anybody, and you know that. You're my best friend, and you just fucked me over."

CHAPTER 20

"Reid, pack up. You're leaving." Once again, I had to get cuffed from my wrist to my ankles. But instead of me riding in a prison bus, I was put into a transport van, since I was the only one leaving.

I can't see nothing through these back windows, I thought. *I don't know why they act like a person that's chained up like this can do anything just by being able to see outside. I'ma just stretch out and take a nap until we stop, since I have no idea where we going.*

Every time you're transferred to a new facility, you have to sit in the holding tank until you're processed, which can take a while. I was brought to another medium-custody prison, but this place had a minimum-custody facility across the street from it. Even though I was intensely hurt, I had to focus as best I could to get acclimated to my new environment and find a center in all the chaos. I had lost a significant amount of weight due to me being in the county plus being depressed, so I was a little on the light side. When I got to my new living unit, I ran into a few people I remembered from when I first started doing my time. I knew that I was getting closer to getting home. It was May, and even after everything that happened, I still wanted to wish Gabrielle a happy Mother's Day. I emailed her and went on about my day.

Thank you, what prison are you in now?

If she wanted to, she could just look that up online. But I let her know and left it at that. A few days later I got another email from her.

I apologize for being reckless with your feelings, I'm just stressed out with having to do everything on my own. I need my friend back.

I couldn't waver from her. I knew she was the one for me. I didn't want to add any extra pressure on her, so I put my emotions aside and continued to be supportive of her, knowing that one day we would figure everything out. In the back of my mind, I thought, *How can you be taking care of bills and everything on your own when you're supposed to have a man in your life who you claim you love and whose kid you're about to have?* I knew that, whoever this person was, she was not happy in that relationship and was just accepting what she had to since she didn't have much support. We emailed once every few weeks. I didn't like it, but what could I do? She had all the power in our relationship. I had to allow things to continue the way they were.

Why haven't I heard from you since my birthday? How are you? Me I feel like I can't keep on track for nothing like I don't know what's wrong with me. I barely find and pay a sitter to watch the kids while I work, it's hard. Anyway do you have a little money you can send me? I'm behind on bills as always. If not it's fine. I love you write back I need you to have my back it's crazy no one have my back like you as I sit and think about it. It's crazy.

Now, any other man would be like, *She's taking advantage of the situation. Fuck her.* But I loved Gabrielle and would never just leave her hanging, so I sent her what I had in my account at the time. Did I feel like I was being taken advantage of? To a degree, yeah. But it was only because of how she had been treating me lately. I knew the love between us was real, but I also knew it was complicated, especially with me being in prison. *Am I making excuses for her behavior?* I wondered. *Or could it be that the passion that I have for her has established an understanding of the specifics of our situation? Or maybe I'm just a pawn in Gabrielle's game? Only time will tell.*

After I sent her a message letting her know that I was sending her what I had, she replied back thanking me and telling me she was moving to Georgia with her mom. *Can you please find time to call me I really need to hear your voice and hear your wisdom. From the bottom of my heart thank you for always being a letter away you never leave me hanging like I'm crying as I write this at 5:50am God is why you're in my life you're one of the good I don't know why I pushed you away I'm sorry I just need you to be my friend again I love you you're such a good person I told you it was always me not you.*

During our phone call, I didn't do much talking. I just sat back and listened to her express how she was feeling. When she first said she was moving out of state, it didn't really register. But once I heard it come out of her mouth, I was shook. All of a sudden, I felt disconnected from her.

After the call, I sent her an email expressing how it hurt me that I couldn't be there for her. *I wanted to ask you, once I got out and out of the halfway house, can I come down there with you and the kids?* I couldn't see my life without Gabrielle, and no matter where she was, I wouldn't let anything come in between us.

The message I received was another heartbreaking blow.

It's okay the father of my child is going to help, and we are getting back together yes I'm pregnant. I know you are going to be mad and I'm not having an abortion. Fact of the matter is I only look at you as family and I thought long and hard before I told you. You say you can't be around me and be my friend so maybe I do have to cut all ties as much as I want a friend out of you, I don't want to lead you on and have you thinking it's more than it is. I have love for you I'm not in love with you, I'm in love with the father of my child and I'm going to make things work with him I hope you understand. I don't need you stressing trying to help me out I got this. Thanks for always being a friend sorry I couldn't be more. Love always Gabrielle.

I can't be reading this right, I thought. *What does she mean the father of her child is going to help her? If that was the case, then why the fuck did she just reach out to me asking for money? I don't know what type of games she playing, but I'ma have to cut all communication with her at this point. I could accept her two children because they were already here before we got to this point, but another one, like this? I couldn't accept that. If she have that baby then we are going to be completely done. I probably wouldn't totally turn my back on her, but I know I won't be able to be there for her like I would want to.*

CHAPTER 21

A few months went by, and I couldn't help but think about how the love of my life was having a child with another man. Plus she said she was in love with him. I wondered how she could be in love with someone so fast. But I had to just let things unfold however they were. Even though I felt like a part of me was missing, I knew I would have to learn how to continue with this empty feeling, because nothing could replace Gabrielle. I would forever feel incomplete and heartbroken.

It's nice out here today, I thought. *I'm looking forward to being able to go outside and not have to see barbed wire or crazy high fences. Being able to do pull-ups at a park or beach instead of on a prison yard would be a lot more therapeutic. A lot of time has passed since I've been away, and there's only so much preparation I can do when it comes to getting released. But as long as I stick to my plans and don't waver, I should be okay.*

The sun was beaming, and I hadn't brought my sunglasses, so I went back to my unit. On the way, I stopped to check my email.

I had an abortion if you care to know.

I had to lean back in the seat for a minute as I began to ponder what I was seeing on the screen. *Why would she do that when she said she was in love with the father, and they were getting back together?* I was doing my best to manage doing the remainder of my time without her, but my heart did wonder if she was okay. I sent a message asking just that.

Bittersweet but I'll be ok.

I felt there wasn't anything else to say, so I replied back saying, *Ok well I'm here if you need me.*

I left it alone from there but later that night I got an email from her saying, *Whatever.*

At first it didn't bother me, but then as I got to thinking on it, I felt disrespected. *What does she mean, whatever?* So I replied to her message.

I know my past efforts have gone unnoticed and my words have fallen on deaf ears but I have never given you a reason to doubt me when it comes to being there for you and having your back when you need me so you can chill out with all that whatever shit.

Even after I sent her that message, something was still pushing me to call her. At first, I wasn't budging, but the force inside me gained control, and I made the call.

"Hello," she answered.

"So what's yo problem?"

"You're just like the rest of these dudes out here. You don't love us."

Whatever else she said didn't even matter, because after she said that I couldn't keep my composure. "You a stupid bitch." I wasn't into disrespecting females, and I immediately felt bad once I said what I said, especially since I knew at the end of the day I still loved her.

She gasped. "Apologize to me."

"Apologize to you for what?"

"For disrespecting me."

"Gabrielle, you disrespect me all the time."

"But I don't never call you out of your name, Brandon. Now apologize to me."

I dropped the phone down and gathered my thoughts. Whatever was between me and her was getting out of control.

"Look, you know I'm sorry for calling you out yo name. But pay attention to what you sayin'. I don't care about you and the kids? That's crazy, don't fix yo lips to say no shit like that to me no more."

That night, we talked for two hours straight. She broke everything down for me.

"I feel like I'm having a baby with someone who I can't see myself being with."

"What do you mean? I thought you said you had an abortion. Are you still pregnant?"

"Yes, Brandon, I am."

"Why did you lie?"

"I set the appointment, but I just didn't go. It's just a lot. I feel that he got what he wanted, after doing what he felt he had to in order to get it, and basically now it's fuck me and my kids. Then I found out he was lying the whole time and he had a total separate life, and I know I can't trust 'um. I know I'm not capable of taking care of another child on my own. I can barely take care of the two I have, and with him not being trustworthy I know I won't have the support I need. I just wish you were here, Brandon."

Deep down, I was crushed and mad. She had literally

cut me off for this dude and had no regard for my feelings. She even went to the extent of throwing the relationship in my face. Having to listen to the woman I loved more than anything tell me that she was pregnant by another man was a lot to handle.

But I could tell in her voice that she needed me. She was confused and didn't know what to do. She confided in me, and she needed me to have her back and guide her. I knew her having another child at this moment wasn't ideal. Not only did she not want to be with this person, but she would be dependent on him to be supportive of the child, and from what she told me, that wouldn't be a good judgment call. "At the end of the day, you have to do what's best for you," I told her. "I would say get the abortion before you're too far along and that's not an option, but only you know what decision you can truly live with. Everything is right there for you, but a decision has to be made, regardless of how you feel right now."

I knew Gabrielle could be unpredictable at times, but I couldn't believe she lied in her email. She knew how to manipulate a situation when she wanted, and that's not how you do somebody that loves you. If she wanted to know if I still cared, she just should have asked, not lied about it. I had to acknowledge the fact that she might follow through and have the baby. Deep down, I knew I would hate her if she did that. I would still be there for her, but I didn't know how.

She sent me an email two days later saying that she really got the abortion and that she felt numb but was okay. I sent her an encouraging email and let her know that I would call her in a few days once I got more phone time, since we had used it all during our two-hour conversation. The next time we spoke on the phone, she said something that caught me off guard.

"Are you happy now?"

"Happy about what?"

"You said you wasn't fuckin' wit me if I had that baby, so are you happy now?"

I was stuck for a minute. "It's not like that, it would have killed me if you had that baby, but I still would have been there when I got out."

CHAPTER 22

"William called me trippin' about talking to you. He had this theory, saying he think that you out already and just not making it known, and he feel like we fuckin' around. Then he was like he'd do something to both of us if he found out we had something goin' on. Maybe we should stop talkin', because I'm not tryna deal with the drama."

"What do you mean, maybe we should stop talkin'? I don't know why you keep allowing somebody else to dictate what we got going on. One minute you wanna love me, then once somebody come around and feel some type of way, you wanna switch yo tune. I'm standing firm on what I'm standing for, and I'm not about to keep this back-and-forth shit goin' wit you."

"Well, you don't have to keep goin' back and forth wit me. I been tellin' you that I don't wanna deal wit no drama behind us doin' what we doin'. I'm not tryna hear none of that shit you talkin' about. This man callin' me and threatenin' me, and I don't have time for it. You don't hear all the shit he be sayin' to me. Fuck him, and fuck you too."

"What you just say to me?"

"You heard what I said, Brandon. Fuck you." *Click.*

"Hello? Hello?"

I don't know what her problem is with thinking it's cool to hang up the phone on me, but I'ma check her ass about that shit. I hate when she get in this type of mood off of someone else's energy. Now can't no type of sense be talked into her.

I called back. "So what's yo problem wit hanging the phone up on me? You gettin' outta control wit dat shit."

"I told you I wasn't tryna hear nothing you had to say. Stop calling my phone back-to-back like that before I block you. If I hung up on you then that's a clear sign that I don't wanna talk to you right now."

"I don't know who you think you talkin' to, but Gabrielle, you better check yo attitude. I'm calling you back so we can resolve the issue and talk it out, like adults do. You do know adults talk through whatever differences they have, right? Only kids run away from their issues."

"Well I said I don't feel like talking to you right now. You can just call me later, since you wanna talk to me so bad."

I really don't know what her problem be sometimes. As soon as somebody come around questioning her about me then she wants to start acting crazy. I can't wait to see her ass in person so I can let her know I'm not tolerating no disrespect, especially when I hold her in such high regard. First it was her hanging up on me, and then she made that blocking me comment. I don't want to have to fuck her up when I get outta here. I know my not being physically there plays a huge role as to why she can't stand her ground, but that's still no excuse for her to be acting the way she do. I know William would have a problem with our connection no matter if me and her were just friends, but since Gabrielle isn't his woman, what she do shouldn't be none of his concern. All he should be concerned with is assisting her with taking care of David. I'ma make a call real quick to see if William been telling people some of the same shit he been telling Gabrielle, but not on this jail phone.

I made my way around the unit but couldn't find who I was looking for. "Ey, any of y'all seen D?"

"Yeah he in the kitchen."

"Aight, good looking."

Walking through the door to the kitchen, I saw D at the microwave cooking up some fried rice. He had the whole table covered with seasonings, packs of mackerel and chicken with white rice and Asian noodles.

"You must be cooking for everybody in yo room tonight?"

"Yeah, it's my roommate's birthday so I told 'um I'd look out. What's going on?"

"You still got yo joint?"

"You already know. You need to use it?"

"Just for a minute. I need to make a call that I don't feel comfortable making on a recorded line."

"Alright, let's step out the back door to the kitchen."

After we got out of the view of any cameras, he passed me his cell phone and I went to my room to make my call.

What type of phone this is? I wondered. *It's crazy how phones have evolved since I was out. I guess flip phones are a part of the Stone Age now. Even the concept of not having buttons on the phone is wild. Everything is all on one screen with all these different portals that they call apps that are basically different worlds in your phone. Hearing about these phones is one thing, but using them is something else.*

I called one of William's friends. "What's going on?" I asked.

"Shit man, just chillin'."

"Do you even know who dis is?"

"Nah, not really."

"Dis Cash."

"My baby, what's poppin'? You out?"

"Something like that. What's going on?"

"Man, nothin' really, just doing what I can to get some shit in order."

"As long as you standing firm on yo principles, then everything else will fall in place."

"You right about that."

"So what's the deal with William? He sending threats talkin' about he got an issue with me and Gabrielle talkin'?"

"I doubt he meant that. You know dude be doin' a lot a talkin, he probably just said that in the heat of the moment."

"He speakin' with a lot of assurance about a place he's never stepped foot in."

"Man, you know he be sayin' shit that don't make no sense."

"Just take care of yoself, and I'ma get at you later. Delete this number."

"Aight, I will. If you need anything—clothes, whatever—I got you."

When I made it back to the kitchen, D was gone. I took a quick glance outside and didn't see him there, so I went to his room.

"Good lookin' on knat, I appreciate it."

BEAUTIFUL CONSEQUENCES

"You already know, cuz, anytime."

It was starting to get late, and I wanted to get my shower out of the way so I could get ready to take it in for the night, but I checked my email before I did.

This is why we can't be together and I can't be fucking wit you, William just called me screaming in the phone talking even crazier than he was before. Keep my name out yo mouth.

She still hasn't learned about talking crazy to me, I thought. I wrote my reply in the room that night and sent it out in the morning.

Keep yo name out my mouth? What the fuck I tell you about talking to me like that? I don't know who you think I am, but I promise you, respect is a must and that is something you will show me at all cost. You be attempting to blame me for everything. I told yo ass way back in the day, don't be bringing my name up in nothing the two of you got going on and what you do? Got to running yo mouth and told him thank God for me because he ain't shit. That's why he got something to say now, you gave him fuel. When you felt like people was being funny towards your son or felt some type of way, I told you just get the blood test so that chapter would be closed. You cried to me about that shit and I just said stay focused, do the best you can, get the test and if all else fails when I'm out I got you. You know when I'm out you don't have to worry about nothing. Don't try to act like I just be running my mouth either. You have told me plenty of stuff he has said about us and me, even sent me text messages and I didn't say shit just to keep the two of you from arguing. I shouldn't have made that call and that's my fault, I can admit that. You hanging up the phone on me and the blatant disrespect has gotten out of control. I said when I got my hands on some money I would send it so just send me an address I can send it to and we can stop talking from this point.

Afterthought: Gabrielle how long have we been rocking, eight years? And in the next months to come when I'm out it will be pushing nine years, you're tripping right now. Before I even came in when he was like "stop talking to her, I don't know why you trust her" I told him whatever you two got going on doesn't have anything to do with me and her relationship. If you notice it's been like this for years, one minute he's trying to tell me not to talk to you, then he's telling you not to talk to me. If me and you were going to stop talking because of him then don't you think it should have been at the beginning not eight years later? If he's aware we haven't stopped talking after all this time then he really knows that us not talking is not going to happen. If we had allowed him to dictate our relationship we would have never found each other, we knew each other but I don't believe what we share and the connection we have, I don't see either of us finding it in other people.

Something kept us together after all this time, there was plenty of things going on in both of our lives throughout the years but somehow we stayed together. When we were separated the universe brought us back together again, something kept you with me, you should think about that. One of our last conversations you said "you don't know why you keep coming back to me." I know why just like you do. You have never felt the love from no other man in your life that you feel from me and in your heart you know that. If you want to cut me off go ahead and do what's best for you. If you don't want to deal with me OK but at the end of the day, mark my words "the universe will bring us back together again." You know why? Because we *are meant to be and are supposed to be in each other's life, we are the pieces that fit in each other's puzzle in life, watch what I tell you. I'ma fall back and let shit play out again and watch how it unfold just like I said it would. When you decide you want to come back home to daddy where you belong, I want a fucking apology Gabrielle.*

That's some low shit to say, that we wouldn't be here if I wasn't in jail, if I was there for you when I was out even when no one wanted me to then why wouldn't I have continued to be there. There is nothing that anyone can tell you that me and you haven't already talked about and that's the honest truth. When that topic came up what did we say, that we didn't know if we would be here or wouldn't be here but we both knew that we would have still been in each other's life no matter what. Since I'm in jail and love and value you, I'm wrong? But the dudes that's out there free, that don't care about you and don't value you are right? If you can agree with them then you right baby, they right, you got it. You should look at that philosophy different. All I know is regardless of everything in a matter of months I'll be out and if you don't value what we have then so be it.

That was really all I had to say at that point. I was tired of fighting for us on my own. Every time somebody had a problem with us, she would close me out and leave. I didn't think she understood what she put me through. She replied back saying she was sorry for disrespecting me, but she only wanted to remain friends. I wasn't trying to hear that. From this moment there would be no more talk from me about us being together. If she wanted me to play the role of her best friend, I would do just that for now. But once I was out and situated, she would have to deny me at my every attempt, because I would never give up on the love we shared and my desire to be with her. My love wouldn't allow me to waver, and that would be something she would have to understand.

CHAPTER 23

I want to apologize for how I came at you in my last message, I'm just stressed out because no one is really helping me and everybody is out for themselves. I want you to stay focused and don't let me throw you off track. I feel you have so much to offer the world and deserve a woman that will give you all she has to offer, I just feel I'm not it. We are best friends and I value that no matter what we argue about.

I hated how she always tried to make it seem as though she didn't love me or didn't want to be with me. I knew that wasn't true, but just hearing her talk like that irritated me to the fullest.

I was working on a crew from the facility that went into the community to work. We mainly cut down hazard trees, put them into piles, and burned them. On this particular day, we were working in St. Paul, not too far from where Gabrielle lived. As we went from location to location, I thought about her, wondering what would be the odds of me seeing her, and as the universe would have it I got that chance. An opportunity presented itself, and I was able to go to her apartment. *So this is it!* The main entrance door didn't even appear to be locked, and I didn't have to buzz to get in. I didn't like the fact that anybody could just walk in here like that. Walking up the stairs to her door, I started to feel beads of sweat forming on my forehead, and my heart started pounding. I froze for awhile as I stared at the numbers on her door. "Brandon, shake it off. You acting like we not on a time crunch." *Knock, knock, knock.*

I stood there in complete shock, thinking, *I hope she's here. I look crazy in these work clothes, and I didn't want this to be the way we seen each other after all these years, but fuck it.* I knocked some more, but she didn't answer. I had some pen and paper just in case. I wrote a note, saying, "I came by to check on you. I knocked a few times but got no answer. It's crazy how we missed each other, and my time is short. Love, Brandon."

I slid the note under her door and headed back to where the work crew was. I wanted to see her so bad, but she could've been anywhere.

She emailed later, saying she got the note. *I'm too mad, it's 6:38pm I just got home I went to get my mom today which usually I don't do. I get David from the recreation center at 6 and Aaliyah off the school bus at 3. I'm so mad and sad I could cry. You know it's snowing so heavy here so I didn't want to drive in the snow it took so long and traffic sucked. But I'm home now going to relax this weekend snuggled watching movies and tv shows. What's going on with you? What's new? Reply ASAP big head.*

All day I couldn't help feeling the excitement of almost being able to hold her in my arms. I knew the time was slowly approaching for the harmonious thoughts I had about us to become reality. I didn't like her and the kids living in that building. Once I got out, if she was still there, then I would have to contribute to them moving out. I felt even if I had to live in a studio apartment just to have extra money to help her pay for a better place I would. Words could only get you so far, so I knew once I was out and she started to see that all the things that I said when I was away were true and I didn't flake on anything, she would truly understand. Until then I had to count down until my release.

CHAPTER 24

I was deep in my feelings one day and decided to send Gabrielle an email to express my thoughts.

A vision I had:

Last night, we got a chance to talk and express ourselves about everything without holding anything back. During this process I began to rub your feet and as you talked, I slowly sucked your toes. Then I unclothed you down to your bra and panties and asked you to lay flat on your stomach so I could give you a massage. I unsnapped your bra, and you obliged by removing it completely and I set it to the side. We continued to talk as I glided my hands to the spots that I felt needed attention and were tense from your shoulders to your upper back, to the middle down to your lower area. As I caressed your tender spots, I placed gentle kisses on each spot after I massaged it. I placed a kiss on your neck and then I licked and sucked on it just a little, then kissed on your shoulder but then I bit on it gently, then I made a trail of kisses from the top of your back all the way down your spine to your ass. I pulled your panties down just a little to reveal where your split begins, then I kissed your ass right at the split and stuck my tongue in between your cheeks and slowly made a trail from your ass to the top of your neck. (As I did so it sent chills through your body and you couldn't help but shake.) Then I kissed the back of your neck. I passed you your bra and you put it back on (I'm trying *to be good) so we could continue our conversation. Time seemed to be keeping up with us because without us realizing it, it was the early hours of the morning and we were both tired. We laid in bed together in each other's arms in our underwear, and we kissed and said goodnight. You laid your head on my chest and we fell asleep.*

This morning, we wake up, and we both feel so relaxed and rejuvenated. We say good morning as we both start moving around. We're both thinking the same thing: "I've never felt so comfortable and safe with anybody like this before." Then a feeling of gratitude and security runs through both of us as we head to the bathroom. We brush our teeth and look at each other in the mirror sometimes just to see how the other does it. As we finish, I gently put your hand into mine as I turn on on the shower and set it at a nice temperature. I ask you to turn around so I can take off your bra. You do as I ask, then I unsnap it and you turn back around as I take your bra off and I set it on the floor. As your breasts are exposed, I think, "They're perfect." So I kneel down, but instead of putting one of your nipples in my mouth like I so badly want to, I just go down to your panties. Instead of using my hands to pull them down I use my teeth, and with you being the voluptuous woman that I love, I have to make my way around gradually, bringing your panties down slowly. Once I get them down to your ankles, you slip each leg out and I set them next to your bra. You see I'm aroused, and while I'm holding your hand to assist you in the shower, you stop me. In a seductive voice, you say, "Let's get these boxers off you." So you pull my boxers down over my hard dick, and then I assist you in the shower and get in behind you. I grab a clean washcloth and lather it up with body wash. I start to wash you from your ears to your neck, down to your breasts. Both of your nipples are hard at this point, so I make sure to be gentle. I make my way down your stomach and wash the sides and your belly button. I rinse the washcloth and lather it up again before I make my way down to your "walls of honey." I ask you, "How do you want me to wash her?" And you attempt to take the washcloth from me, but I resist and say, "I'm doing this, so tell me how." You tell me, so I wash your pussy and then your thighs, legs, and feet. I stand back up as the water rinses off the front of your body and ask you to turn around, and you do so. I start to wash your neck and your back and then work my way down to your ass. I start on the outside and then spread one cheek at a time to make sure I get in between both sides. You start to rinse off the back of your body. My dick is rock hard, and as I start to grab another washcloth you ask me, "What you doin'?" You take the washcloth from me and grab the same washcloth I just used on you and say, "Let me do it." You start to wash me up from my ears, neck, chest, shoulders, my back, my abs, you even wash my dick and balls for me. Then I rinse off and we get out the shower. We walk into the bedroom, and I start to dry you off, then you take the towel and dry me off too. I go to the counter and ask you which lotion is your favorite. I grab it and ask you to lay on your stomach on the bed. I start to lotion your back, then make my way down to your ass and lotion up both cheeks and then kiss each one. Then I ask you to flip over and sit up on the edge of the bed. You sit up and I start to lotion your upper chest, your stomach, your thighs, legs, and feet. As I come back up I notice your walls of honey, so I look at you and ask, "Can I taste you?" And you say, "Yes, baby." Before I start, I kiss her from top to bottom, and I remember you telling me you like your pussy ate slowly, so I make that my tempo. I start by licking her straight from the bottom to the top and then trace her with kisses, then when I return to the top, I lick her until I get to your entrance and slide my tongue in. As I lick the inside of your walls of honey, I'm making sure to pay attention to your reaction as I try to eat each wall and see which wall is your sweet spot. As I go from your right wall to the top of your pussy, to your left wall down to the bottom, I start to French kiss your pussy like I was kissing you face to face, and from the moans you making and the way you moving your body, I know you like it. Then I insert one finger so I can massage her while I continue to feast on my favorite meal. You're about to cum, and I continue to lick her how you like it until you release all your juices and I gladly swallow every drop you have to offer. Then since I want you to cum for me one more time, I lay on the bed next to you and say, "Come ride daddy face and don't hold back." So with a smile on your face, you straddle mine and ride it until you cum again. Once you're done I get up and we kiss passionately and then I assist you in getting dressed and leave you to your thoughts.

 Don't let me throw us off, we're in a good place right now. I was just giving you what I had envisioned. I love you baby.

 Only Gabrielle could have me this way. I wanted to do things to her and for her that I never thought about doing for no other woman. She had me wide open and I would do anything to please her.

 Hey love bug,

 I hate to hear that your days haven't been so good. You're always so strong I didn't take the time to think how you are physically and emotionally and for that I apologize babe. It's *crazy because just how you're frustrated last week all I kept thinking is how I wish you could hurry up and be free. Like I was almost feeling lonely and mad you were not here for me, then I had to remind myself not to be selfish, I'm out here free while you're being told what to do all the time. You have so much to offer to the world just stay focused and strong for me.*

I am here for you, and you be on my mind just as much I'm sure. David had a good birthday, he got to see his dad and we went to eat. He was so happy to get 2k I swear I played a trick like I couldn't get it, but when I gave it to him, I was the best mom and I love that David is so thankful for the little things. Anyways to that letter you just sent OMG can you say WETTTT I was dropping by the end I SWEAR!!!! You are the sweetest person I know I love that about you, I love how your mind thinks like you know how to treat a woman. It's a must we write a book, like your details are so real I thought it was happening like I could picture it all so vividly. I started work today they're working with me on my schedule until I get Aaliyah in daycare until my mom can get both the kids for me for after school. I feel I can grow into this company, and I am vowing to keep this job and give it my all, if I'm lacking make sure to remind me of my vow! I am trying to focus on me and the kids for now and give you more time and attention that I can. I have been selfish to you when you need me most, if I was there I would be hurt not having you there for me like you always here for me, how can I be better when it comes to supporting you and being here for you to get done with your little time fast and motivated? Anyways I have a prepaid government phone I use for jobs, you can call me tomorrow to talk we just have to limit calls until I get a real phone plan but call me so I can hear your voice please. I'll add some money to my prepaid to talk to you at least fifteen minutes!

 I was glad she liked the message and loved the fact that it made her pussy wet. It let me know that I could still stimulate her sexually even from behind a wall. It was good that David had a good birthday. I knew she was stressing about that. I appreciated that she had recognized how she had been selfish towards me and wanted to do better by me, that's really all I asked for right now. I called that next day and we talked for fifteen minutes. Hearing her voice always did something to me. It just seemed like all the stressful things in life had no meaning when I spoke to her, I felt maybe speaking with me did something for her as well, because she always mentioned how she needed to hear my voice. Her voice was my remedy. I would look at pictures of her and it would calm me down instantly, and seeing her would raise my nature. It was like she controlled my senses. I always wondered what she smelled like and couldn't wait to be able to hold her in my arms and finally be able to look into her eyes so I could truly see if the love that was in my heart was in hers as well.

CHAPTER 25

It was Christmastime, the last one I would spend locked up, and I wanted to do something nice for Gabrielle. I was low on cash and as I was in my thoughts, an ad started on the TV: "Get your loved one the gift that keeps on giving. This year, we are partnering with Pandora to bring you a collection of bracelets with a large variety of charms, so you can customize your bracelet the way you want. Come into your neighborhood KAY jewelry store and ask to see the Pandora section. Every kiss begins with KAY." It was like the TV was reading my mind. *That could be a nice gift for her—even though it's not that expensive, I could always upgrade it later for a better one.* I just wanted to surprise her to let her know that she was always on my mind. Then she could finally have something tangible to remember me by when she looked at it and felt it on her arm. I just had to figure out what charm to get for her bracelet. I wouldn't be able to see it due to the lack of internet access, but I still wanted it to pertain to something memorable. Even before we started having disagreements about our relationship, Gabrielle said that I was her "best and most loyal friend." I hated to be looked at as just a friend to her—I knew that what we had was deeper than friendship—but that the statement she made was true. I could accept that title because, when I heard of people confessing their love to each other or saw people get married on TV, you would hear one or the other say, "You're my best friend." That's how I viewed our bond, as something sacred. So I made an arrangement to have the bracelet sent to her house and picked a charm that represented us being best friends. She sent me an email on Christmas Day asking me to call her the next day so she could hear my voice and update me on the events in her life. Her bracelet would be delivered on that day as well, and I hoped she liked it.

"Hey, did you try to call me earlier?"

"Nah, it must have been one of them other guys you be talkin' to."

"Nope, don't nobody have this number." After a brief pause, she said excitedly, "I got my bracelet today! When I opened my mailbox I thought they had made a mistake because I wasn't expecting anything. You didn't even tell me either."

"It would have spoiled it."

"You know how I hate surprises. I always wanted one of these charm bracelets, but every time I thought about gettin' one, I didn't."

"I'm just glad you like it."

"I love it. It made my day."

CHAPTER 26

It was two days after Valentine's Day, and I still hadn't heard anything from Gabrielle. Even though I couldn't send her a gift, I sent her three emails telling her a romantic story about us. I was about to email her again and tell her how I didn't appreciate us not talking, but I decided to call instead.

"What you doin'?" I asked.

"On my way to Chicago."

I knew something wasn't right. Her energy was off, and I got an uneasy feeling in my stomach. "What you goin' knat way for?"

"Goin' to see my dude."

"Is this the same dude you were just messing wit or someone new?"

"The same one. He gave me a ring, and I'm just tryna figure out the situation I'm in."

"So this is the same dude you said didn't care if you and the kids had money and that you didn't trust?"

"Who are you to judge me?"

"Judge you? I'm just going off what you told me."

"Yeah I said all dat, but I don't want to hear all dat from you."

"Is this why I haven't heard from you?"

After a hard sigh, she said, "Yes, Brandon, that's why. I

read your email and that was too much. Brandon, I can't cross that line. You only like this because you in prison. I have to think about who my child's father is. I don't have feelings for you like that. You have to get out and find you somebody to love, and who will love you back and you can be happy."

"Gabrielle, that's impossible. You make me happy. I'm in love wit you and I don't believe you don't love me."

"Now you acting weird saying that's impossible. I'm tellin' you I love somebody else, and you keep tellin' me how I feel. I hate dat shit."

"I'm just going off what you told me."

"I just need you to stop. If you can't respect my decision, I'm going to block you from my phone and email."

"What . . . Are you serious?"

The prerecorded voice cut in. "You have sixty seconds remaining."

"Yes, I'm serious. I'm pullin' up to where he at, so don't call back."

"Gabrielle, I can't even call you back?"

"No, you can't. Bye."

I tried to call back, but she didn't answer. I made a separate call to someone else to express how I felt, but after a few short words, the impact struck me. I couldn't talk, even though my mouth was wide open. The person on the other line asked if I was okay, and tears began to roll down my face. I wiped my face and finished my call. I couldn't think straight after that. Once again I felt that emptiness inside that only she could fill.

The conversation played back to me like it was on a tape

recorder. She not only judged me for loving her but said I was only like this because I was in prison. Her judging me really hurt, plus blocking me from all communication was torture. She said I was acting weird because I said that it was impossible for me to love somebody else, and that was a crucial blow. She didn't even let me finish so I could explain what I truly meant by the statement I made. Gabrielle was my best friend, and I had fallen in love with her. I had given her my all from behind prison walls—attention, loyalty, encouragement, wisdom, money, love—whatever she needed and wanted I gave without a second thought or hesitation. For her to say I was acting weird was pure insulting. She was my better half, she balanced me out, she was the missing piece to my puzzle.

Then the comment about me only being like this because I was in prison struck a nerve. The "prison love" stereotype was basically a man telling a woman whatever she wanted to hear, all the right things, selling her a falsified fantasy or dream in order to get what he wanted from her—but once he was out, he would leave the woman hanging. I hated having that stigma attached to me, because I knew this was all too real. I couldn't blame her for thinking that at times, because there was a lot on the line, and what if she did take that risk with me just to find out that I didn't truly love her the same once I was out?

The stereotype for guys in prison was bad. We were labeled master manipulators and considered compulsive liars in order to get whatever we wanted to make our time easier. I didn't understand the scrutiny, since people who were free did the same thing, if not to a higher degree. From the things I heard from the outside, it seemed like everybody out there was getting over on everybody.

Most men, if they had a woman who hustled, would be trying to get as much money from her as they could and encourage her to engage in that activity for their benefit. But with me and Gabrielle it was completely the opposite— I could never encourage her to do things like that. Even with my knowledge of what she did sometimes and us not having a title, I still sent her money when I had it. After she told her friend Ashley that I was sending her money, she even said, "I have never heard of no man sending money out from prison. He really love you." Then on top of that, what other man would still support her after she cut him off, got pregnant, and came back? That's genuine love, not no prison shit.

I wanted to address things properly once I was home. I wanted to sit down with Gabrielle's mom, sister, and brother to express how I really felt and to ask for her mother's blessing to marry Gabrielle. Then we could talk to her cousin Porsha just to clear the air with her. I wanted to have a man-to-man conversation with William to let him know that this wasn't out of spite. Then of course I would have a sit down with William's mom and grandmother to enlighten them on my feelings and tell them that I appreciated them giving me a place to come when I was younger to clear my mind sometimes but hoped they could understand that I truly loved Gabrielle. I knew that a conscious, mature, and mentally sound person could understand even if they didn't completely agree.

I knew that there was someone in her ear influencing her to break ties to me, and I hated that. It angered me that someone would try to come in between us, but I understood the game. Even with me being in prison, any man in her life would be jealous of our connection and relationship. I was furious with Gabrielle, and her saying she was blocking me only made me even more upset.

The next day I said fuck it. I started a letter that took me two days to finish and came out to six pages. I told her that I wouldn't contact her again and that I was completely cutting ties to her. She kept allowing other people to dictate our relationship and I couldn't honor that. If she wanted to accommodate everybody else, then she could fully do that now without me in her life. Being her friend like this would be almost impossible. She had given me her word that we would try being together, and that she loved me just as much as I did her, yet it was looking like we were going our separate ways for good.

CHAPTER 27

I put my good-bye letter to Gabrielle in the mailbox, but it wouldn't go out until the next morning. I felt that I needed to get everything off my chest and just let things be. I had been in deep thought all day, and even though I was intensely hurt, for some reason it was like I didn't know if my course of action was the right choice. I rarely ever talked to anyone about my personal issues, but for some reason this one person came to mind that I felt I should speak with. His name was Mr. Washington, and he was a janitor in the unit. Our relationship began with us having conversations in the morning before I went out to work. In our first few encounters, his humor was kind of odd, but I knew it was his way of attempting to feel me out. As time progressed, things shifted. He would say things like, "Don't give up now, you've come too far," or he would encourage me to stay focused, follow my dreams, and leave the past in the past. Breaking out of my comfort zone, I approached Mr. Washington and broke down the situation to him about everything, including the letter I just put in the mailbox cutting all ties to Gabrielle.

"Brandon, if she has been there for you all this time, you can't just give up now. Listen to me: you should take that letter back. You probably said some things in there that could really hurt her. You don't know everything she's going through. She's probably hurting, and for you to just give up on her would probably break her. If she's your best friend, you have to be understanding. You have to look at it like this: you're the man and she's a woman. You're the stronger vessel.

"It's like tug of war. The child's father is probably in her ear making her feel bad, and even though he didn't want her, he don't want you to have her. Or maybe it's a different guy. You got to realize if the two of you are that close, then those other guys are jealous of you. She has been with you all this time—she chose you and they know that. They could be threatening her or even beating on her, and you're not out there to protect her. If you really love her, you don't give up. You fight for her. But just be smart. Get out, get your life in order, stack you some money, get you a place and a car, and still be there for her. Believe me, she's going to call you one day and want to spend some time with you.

"Brandon, take that letter back. If you don't, you could regret it for the rest of your life."

After careful consideration, I felt a new sense of understanding for the situation. My mind drifted to a lot of me and Gabrielle's prior conversations, about how she loved me for being myself and never leaving her hanging. How she felt nobody had her back, understood her struggle, or knew her the way I did. How for a while when guys tried to talk to her, that she would compare them to me and instantly turn them down because she felt that I had shown her what a real man was all about and didn't want to settle for less anymore. How after I expressed to her how I wanted to talk to her family and ask her mom for her blessing

BEAUTIFUL CONSEQUENCES

to marry her, it made her cry because she said that no man in her entire life had shown her the type of love that she felt from me. How she told me that the reason she thinks she runs away from me is because my love is so real that it scares her. How when I told her I was talking to another woman consistently a while back, she said she was jealous and didn't want nobody to take her spot. How she wanted me to be a constant figure in her children's life. How she couldn't wait until I came home so we could do fun stuff together with the kids and she could just vent to me about everything.

Once I came back to the present moment, my heart began to talk to me. It was like a compass that always led in her direction. I knew what I wrote in that letter wasn't true. I couldn't cut ties from her if I wanted to. If she called me and said "come," I would be on my way.

This was Gabrielle's pattern with me. When she was getting to the point that she wanted to give her heart to me, she would start acting irrational and push me away. It was her defense mechanism. But in my heart I knew that when she had told me she loved me, it was all real. The relationship between her and her ex wouldn't last because her heart was with me, she was just too scared to admit it.

From behind a wall, things got filtered. But in the flesh, a person couldn't hide and the authentic self would be present. If she could honestly look me in my eyes, tell me that she didn't love me and didn't have any deeper feelings for me, then I would remove myself from her life and leave her be. But I had to look into her eyes to see the truth. Mr. Washington was right: I wasn't out there to provide and protect her. I knew all I had to do was check her ass one good time and lay the law down, then all the back-and-forth shit would stop. But I had to do that once I was out in person.

I went to retrieve the letter that I put in the mailbox earlier. The female sergeant working was cool and didn't have a problem getting the letter out the box for me. "What, did you mail a letter to the wrong girl or something?"

"Nah, I just wrote some things that wouldn't contribute to a good purpose."

"Sometimes, if we just sleep on something, we feel different the next day."

CHAPTER 28

After getting the letter back, I just threw it on my bunk and left it there. Two days had gone by, so I reread it to see what I felt about what I originally wrote. I wouldn't call or email her, but I did feel that something had to be said. My mind started to envision possible scenarios like, what if her ex saw the bracelet and questioned her about it? What if she told him it was from me, and I was in jail? Any man would be like, *He's sending gifts from prison, this must be serious.* Yet only a man who doesn't have her best interest at heart would try to come in between her and her best friend. I understood that I was locked up and this dude was free, so he had the upper hand for now. I wrote another letter, but this one was only half a page, and my mind was clearer when I wrote it.

First, I would like to apologize for not being there for you like I should I know me being in here has taken a toll on both of us and I know that I don't know everything that's going on out there. I know that you're in a lot of pain baby and are still hurting from prior things that you've been through but I'm here Gabrielle. My job and obligation to you is to be loving, supportive, loyal, protective and above all else understanding of you regardless of people, conditions and circumstances. I gave my word and I'll never break that when it comes to you. Just remember don't ever give up on me, because I'll always have your back no matter what.

I didn't think that this guy had access to her mailbox, so I imagined she would get the letter. But even if she didn't, at least I put it into the universe. With that doubt and knowing it needed to be eliminated, I concentrated my thoughts on her receiving and reading it. My mind started to shift into an "Art of War" perspective. I understood that there was a possibility that me and Gabrielle might not talk for a while, so I had to get things in order.

I thought about her friend Ashley. She was all for me and Gabrielle being together, and she knew our history and didn't judge us. So I figured if I didn't speak to Gabrielle around the time I got released, I would have to track down Ashley. I would have to make her my ally so I could check up on Gabrielle through her and to get her to pass word to Gabrielle when I was out. I still had a number for Ashley but didn't know if it was still on, and I wouldn't try to call until I was released. Hopefully I wouldn't have to.

I also needed to get info on this dude Gabrielle was dealing with. I didn't plan on doing anything to anybody, but I still needed to know who I was dealing with. Then I thought about William threatening Gabrielle. Even though he never followed through on his threats, he could pull it on her because she had no one to protect her. If he ever put his hands on Gabrielle, I would step in, and whatever happened I was willing to accept.

At that moment I knew I had to get even more focused than before. I was cutting off all communication to the outside world: no calls, no emails, nothing. It was time to isolate myself and prepare for the most important fight of my life. I would have my out date soon and needed to be sharper than ever. I was in love, and if I had to go against the whole world and win in order to have Gabrielle and for us to be happy, then I hoped the world was ready.

CHAPTER 29

All is fair in love and war. This was my new philosophy. I knew that prison had influenced me. I had not only grown but evolved into the being I was, with a thirst for seeking enlightenment of higher proportions. I didn't think my war for Gabrielle's love would involve guns blazing, sacrifice, and death—I just had to outsmart the people trying to come in between us. My old self would have been excited about physical war, because back then I was strictly impulsive, and I hadn't been working the strongest muscle I had—my brain.

In prison, I had read the book *The Secret*. It was a collection of stories of how intense mental focus reaped the exact results that the mind portrayed. You not only had to think about what you desired, but you had to speak on it, with actions to match and no doubt in your mind, just pure conviction of knowing. I took my time shifting past the doubtful thoughts and focused intensely on what I wanted and spoke about those things with such conviction, like I knew what I wanted would manifest physically. I didn't waver my aim, not once, and as time went by, it seemed that whatever I asked for or wanted to know came right to me. At first it seemed weird, but I tried again, and again what I wanted manifested itself. I had felt an energy inside me that I'd never had before.

I needed to get that focus back. I was letting what Gabrielle said and being in prison cut me off from my power. I had to focus on the friendship and bond we had, how we both felt we needed each other. There was no doubt that we loved each other, but I was letting things cloud my vision of what we truly shared. I was having flashbacks of those conversations. I was crushed that we weren't talking at all, but no matter how hurt I was, I had to allow things to play out and have faith in the love we shared and that the universe would bring us back together. I had to remove the negative energy from my mind and body, and after my daily workout I felt a lot better.

Since coming to prison, I had become more spiritual and in tune with "The Most High," and even though I wasn't into organized religion, a religious scripture came to mind that I liked: "Faith without works is dead." I settled and concentrated my mind, held an image of me and Gabrielle together at the front, then said a silent prayer for her and the kids. The Most High knew my heart and knew that I loved her purely.

Had I not come to prison, it probably would have taken me a lot longer to reach this point mentally. I used to give people the benefit of the doubt without earning it, give blind loyalty without mutualism, and let conventional standards, stigmas, and the opinion of the masses dictate my life, when really I was the true creator of my own destiny. My own ignorance and limited thinking made me to live in fear of crossing imaginary lines that were set by people to keep me in bondage with them. Allowing this kept me miserable and unhappy, which in turn closed off my mind to things that could bring me happiness and serve my greater good.

Now I only really cared about me and Gabrielle's relationship. I would address everything else in due time, but I wasn't letting her go without putting up a fight.

CHAPTER 30

You would think that, with the time getting closer to my release, I would be overjoyed, but it was the opposite. It seemed that everyone else at the time was more excited about my release than I was. A lot of people wanted to collaborate with me and have me in their circumference, which wasn't a bad thing if it was genuine. Sometimes I would wonder what made people look at me with such high regard. What did they see that attracted them to me? What was their angle? Everyone had a reason why they formed alliances and got into relationships. I knew power was based purely on your contacts and your vision on how to utilize people correctly for specific tasks. Everyone had a specific role to play, and when you had your team together and the right individuals in their tailored positions, everyone prospered. I needed to get out and take my alliances at a moderate pace. There would be a lot of things pulling for my attention, so I would take my time deciphering what was what and who was who.

I sent a card to Gabrielle a few weeks later, even though I knew I probably would get no reply. I still had to put my love for her in the universe. *These weeks without speaking are turning into months!* I thought. *I'ma write her one more time and send a card with it. After this, I'm not contacting her again.*

Mi Amor,

I have to get all this off my chest. I've been doing a lot of thinking as you can imagine, and I need to address a few things. Me and you have come a long way, a really long way. I never thought I would be where I am today, confessing my love for you and fighting for your love with all I got from behind these walls but that's exactly what I'm doing. You have brought something out of me that I didn't know was there. The strength that your love has instilled in me for me to endure the things that I have with you and experience the pain I have felt from you, it amazes me how I still love you as much as I do but I know why.

You say you want to cut ties from me, you say you don't love me, and that I'm only like this because I'm in prison. so let me check yo ass real quick about a few things. Even though we don't have an ideal past I know what's between us is real and we have an ideal future. I fucking love you and this is not no prison shit. Love is not something that comes easily for me, so stop putting me in the same category with the rest of these dudes because me and you both know I'm not like them.

You said I'm weird because I said it's impossible for me to love someone else the way I do you. I fell in love with my best fucking friend, of course I know I could never love someone else the way I do you. Then you had the nerve to say that maybe you keep coming back to me because you're lonely. Let me tell you something, you bet not ever come out yo mouth and say no stupid shit like that to me again. You only fucking with them dudes out there because you're lonely. You keep coming to me because you know that I really love yo ass and I do anything for you to make you happy.

BEAUTIFUL CONSEQUENCES

Throughout the years I have had different women in my life and you have had different men in yours but we both came to the conclusion that nobody cares and loves us through whatever like we love each other. The men out there don't want to see you happy and want you miserable like them. I know my all from in here wasn't good enough for you but that's nothing compared to my all when I'm out there. I'ma show you what real love is, and once you see it for yourself and feel it, I want a fucking apology Gabrielle for even thinking that this is some prison love shit.

What's mine is yours and you're never alone as long as I'm breathing. Don't ever forget that.

P.S. Don't ever let another man question you about me EVER. Don't ever let no other man come in between us and compromise your perspective of me. You know better, that isn't for us.

CHAPTER 31

Being separated from Gabrielle was torture. Not being able to feel her presence or hear her voice was the equivalent of being blindfolded or not being able to breathe properly. Something in me told me that she felt the same pain I felt, that something was missing when we were not in each other's life. I tried to do things to feel as though she were still close to me. I looked at pictures that she sent to me and replayed conversations we'd had.

"I'm starting to feel uncomfortable about my weight," she said to me once.

"What do you mean?"

"I got rolls on the side of my stomach, and I don't like that at all. I have completely let myself go."

"All you have to do is start moving around more and incorporate a small exercise routine and you will start to see the weight decline. Do dat and be conscious of what you putting into yo body and I promise you that you'll be okay. Regardless of what yo size is, I'm gone always want you."

"You just saying that now because you not around me all the time. When you come home if I'm too big, you gone leave me high and dry."

"The way you make me feel, I know a few extra pounds

won't turn me off from you. Anyway, I can help encourage you to get where you wanna be. You know I will."

I spent some more time thinking of Gabrielle. When it came to her, I was knocked dizzy by what I called a double-A combo. She had a powerful hold on me, the *allure* she had over me was captivating to the point that she was the only woman that mattered in my world. Not only was the allure she had on me alarming, but I *adored* her.

Her voice: Hearing her voice always did something to me, sometimes it didn't matter what the dynamic was. If she was comforting me, if she was expressing to me how the kids were doing, if I was being supportive after listening to her problems or if we were fighting, no matter what, hearing her voice brought me a sense of gratitude. Hearing her curse me out was better than not hearing her at all.

Her face: I looked forward to seeing her with no makeup on and hair not done, to witness her smile from my efforts would bring me unbelievable joy.

Her features: I couldn't wait to come home so I could look into her eyes. Her lips were luscious and looked like they were just made to say my name.

Her body: She wasn't a skinny woman, but to me she wasn't fat either. She was a voluptuous woman on the thicker side, and I knew I wouldn't be able to get enough of her. She had a mole on her left breast that to me was a beauty mark. After I saw the picture and asked her about it, she said that her mom had moles and knew she would have more as she got older. Her breasts were perfect to me. And her ass looked delicious. I just wanted to bite and suck on each cheek. I thought that by me just coming home I would probably buss a nut just from her sitting on my lap, only because it was her.

Her mental: I couldn't ask for a more perfect connection. We both wanted the same things: someone to be honest, trustworthy, unselfish, understanding, loyal, committed, devoted, strong, courageous, and focused on us. We both needed these attributes in the person we were with but couldn't find it anywhere else but with each other. The only time we argued was when it came to people trying to come in between us or the concept of how people would feel about us being together. Other than that, our relationship couldn't be better.

The way she comforted me: I felt she was the only woman who knew how to take care of me the way I needed to be taken care of.

It was like she was tailor-made for me, her flaws and all. We both even laughed about how much I loved her. She had sent me a message telling me how much she loved me for loving her despite her flaws. I let her know that I didn't care if she had rolls and moles and that her mood swings were accepted in my life. I was a sucker for her love but I didn't care.

One day I was in the cafeteria reading and a shadow formed over me and the book I was reading.

"Brandon, what's the deal, bro?"

"CT, what's going on man? I know you ready to get up outta here. How you feelin'?"

"Man, it's been a long four years, and I'm just ready to put this behind me. I came lookin' for you because I wanted to pass you this astrology book. I was just gon' leave in it the book area, but I figured you would get good use out of it. It's some useful information in there."

"I appreciate that, I'll definitely take it off yo hands. When you get back out there, you just gotta stay focused and maneuver around all the distractions. We know when it comes to this place, its like Motel Six: They gone leave the light on fa you."

"I already know. I don't have time to be comin' back in here under no circumstances. I'ma just stay in my lane and out of everybody else's way. I'ma hit you on JPay once I get situated."

"Do dat. It's good to see you leave. I'm right behind you."

I had never gotten into astrology before. As I started diving into the book, it did have some information about Gabrielle's sign and her personality that made sense. I also started to do research on my own sign to see if the information fit me, and a lot of it did. I studied a lot of information that had to do with her. Reading the astrology book and studying her sign gave me a sense as if I was still in sync with her. I felt that no matter what happened that nothing could keep us apart once I was home.

CHAPTER 32

I had just received the news that I had waited years to hear: I had been accepted into the work release program and would be released in under 120 days. I had been behind a wall for so long that at times I thought that this day would never come. I needed to get my mind properly prepared for my departure. I didn't want everyone to know that I was being released earlier than expected, so I would only inform a select few. After I told my mom and little brothers, I felt that no one else needed to know yet. In order to accomplish what I wanted to do once I was released, I would have to act like I was still in prison, and the only way I could do that was to keep my release as private as possible until I was able to move around on my own terms. I had always imagined telling Gabrielle the good news of me coming home, but I had no access to her and had no way to pass the message even if I wanted to.

"We are all here today to bring these two people together in holy matrimony. If there is anyone in this building that objects to this marriage, speak now or forever hold your peace."

"I object."

As I walk down the aisle with my eyes locked in on Gabrielle, I hear the voices of random people. "Who is that?" "What is he doing?" "Where did he come from?"

"Gabrielle, you can't marry him, not without me letting

you know that I feel I'm the man you should be marrying. I love you unconditionally. I will stick by your side through sickness and in health. I will support you and motivate you in the darkest of times when no one else will, and I will protect you from whatever harm may present itself to you even if I'm hurt in the process. If you can still continue to marry this man knowing that I love you the way I do, then I will go and leave the two of you to live the happy life that you both want. But you have to look me in my eyes and tell me that you don't love me."

This scenario had played in my mind a few times. I knew that when I got out I would do whatever I had to in order to get my point across, even disrupting a wedding if need be. I didn't want it to have to come to that, so I tried my best not to allow myself to think too hard on that outcome. I just hoped that her and the kids were okay and was grateful to know that soon I would be free to pursue her and figure out exactly what was going on.

CHAPTER 33

Hey,
 I know I'm probably the last person you want to hear from but I just can't turn my back on you, I don't feel right. Here's my thing, I wish you could be my best friend without the extra stuff that makes me uncomfortable. I wish you could respect me telling you that I want my friend back not the extra things that don't sit right with me. Idk anyways I hope that you are okay and doing fine, life is too short not to tell you I love you and will always be a friend to you. I just have to remove myself when I'm not comfortable because I don't want to hurt you, I wish you didn't love me how you do.

We hadn't spoken in three and a half months, so of course I was happy to hear from her, but what she said in the message was textbook Gabrielle. I knew she felt the same as I did but hated being caught in the middle of everyone. I didn't know what to say so I didn't respond. A few days later I received another message from her.

I know you read my message and I sent you a stamp to reply so no reason you didn't besides you don't want to talk to me. I will respect that always. I hope you're okay love you and I'm proud of you for all you have accomplished even behind bars, you will do just fine once you come home.

I was still upset with her for how she left months prior and I didn't like her tone in the message. I knew she was so used to me coming when she called, so when I didn't respond she was probably offended. I wanted to ignore her like she had done me for the past three and a half months and not say anything at all, but once again I felt a magnetic pull in my heart that I couldn't ignore. I missed her and even though I was mad I still wondered if her and the kids were safe, so after some careful contemplation I responded.

The queen is upset once again. What did I do this time? I blame myself a little bit because even though I was in here I spoiled yo ass, I gave you everything you ask to the point that you just do what you want to do, like you don't know how to fucking act when dealing with me. Even when you purposely do things to hurt me, I put my pride to the side and do as you ask of me and still stick by you and have your back. Baby, what do you want me to do? My feelings are not going to change because they are REAL, so I won't even comment on that. There is a time and a place for everything, I have questions that I want to ask but I have to wait until I'm home. Then you can look me in my eyes and give me the answers and then we can really figure out how we can move forward, and we will have that chance real soon to where we can sit down and talk. What are you so mad at me about Gabrielle? Don't ever think that I don't want to talk to you because you know that's not the case. I'm hurt and confused, that's all. I haven't heard from you or heard your voice in months, and you know how that affects me. I don't know what's been going on with you or the kids but all I do is pray that you all are safe and keep putting my love for you in the universe. You're so fucking selfish, you don't think about how things affect me after the fact. You don't know what's been going on in here or if I been getting into trouble by losing my cool on the account of how you treat me. Then you got the nerve to still be talking slick (I promise that shit is going to change when I get out) because I took a little minute with my reply. You know how many times I wrote you and got no reply? You're so inconsiderate LOL and I know I'ma be fine when I get home because you're going to be right there with me when I get out. I'm not letting your ass go nowhere I don't know what you think this is. I hope you have a good day, it's really good to hear from you. You know you can talk to me about anything, no matter what we fight about I'm going to always be here for you.

P.S.

Just because I don't jump right when you say so doesn't mean that I'm not going to jump at all. You know I got you, but you got to let me be mad sometimes, look at the shit you be putting me through Gabrielle damn LOL. Also you said you hate that I love you the way I do, be careful saying things like that because if I didn't love you the way I do, just think about how different things would be for the both of us and what we both would have possibly missed out on.

I felt that my response touched on everything that needed to be said then. Some things just had to wait until I was out to be truly expressed, because me being behind bars was distorting the effect of our communication. I knew I would always be her best friend, but I wanted more than that, and I decided that I wouldn't push the issue at this point.

CHAPTER 34

F*inally you reply. I never really thought about things the way you do, I guess I am very selfish and inconsiderate when it comes to you. That is not okay, and I don't think about how things can affect you in jail I hope you are strong enough to not fall into trouble. I know for a fact that you are strong enough Brandon.*

Anyways call me so I can hear your voice and don't take days please big head.

I hadn't heard her voice in a long time, so I was eager to talk to her and know what had happened to switch her perspective.

"What are you doin'?" I asked.

"At work, I'm about to take my break." She brought me up to speed about her daughter's graduation and how she wasn't in a relationship anymore. "How do you know when you were writing me that he wasn't getting the mail and putting his hands on me about that?"

"I had thought about that, and that's why I stopped writing. I didn't think he had access to your mailbox because I had just sent you the bracelet right before we stopped talking, but then I got to thinking like maybe he seen it and it caused a problem."

"He didn't see it because I put it up. I got it on my wrist right now."

"I don't believe you."

"I do."

"So do you want to talk to me about what happen wit him?"

"No. I don't want you to throw it in my face."

We just got caught up on the current events in each other's lives. She asked about one female I used to talk to, and I informed her that I cut her off because I didn't see things going anywhere. My mind started to drift to my out date. Gabrielle still didn't know that I would be home in under a hundred days, so I decided to mess with her.

"I got a surprise for you."

"For real, what is it?"

"I'm not telling you yet."

"Stop playing tell me. I just looked you up and it say you don't get out until next year."

"That's not accurate. They don't put your work release date online."

"So when do you get out, Brandon?"

"I get out in two months. I'm just waiting to figure out which halfway house I'm going to."

"Damn, I'm so excited. Do you need somebody to pick you up?"

"They have an agent give me a ride to the halfway house from here."

"Damn, you got to go straight there?"

"Yeah, but when I first get there, they give me a four-hour pass to get clothes and stuff, so you can come get me and then take me to get a few items."

"Okay, just let me know when so I can take off work

ahead of time. You need to act like you're not out when you come home."

"That's my plan. If I have my way nobody will know I'm out until I'm out of the halfway house." As we continued to talk a thought crossed my mind. A few months back I got access to a cell phone and was able to take a picture and send it to my little brother to keep in his phone. I wanted to be able to compare and contrast when I got out in regard to my physique. I wanted Gabrielle's perspective—she was really the only woman I was attempting to impress—but I looked at myself all the time and really didn't know how others would perceive me. "I took a picture a few months ago and I want to know what you think about it."

"What is it, like a model picture?"

"I guess you can say dat. I just wanna know what you think."

"Okay, I'll be waitin' on it."

After I sent the photo to her, I got a message back.

This was my last stamp & I don't have no money for now I had to pay my care note & what not. Anyways I got the pic OMG I didn't think you looked that good. You look very good sir lol anyways you can call me whenever you feel like it, I miss talking to you already. Hearing your voice made me so happy laughing but serious your body looks great like you been taking care of yourself I'm proud of you. You're looking like a snack for that a whole meal.

Hearing the compliments from Gabrielle gave me the validation that not only was I going to be a force to be reckoned with once I was released into the world on the physique side, but also I was more than appealing to her, and that's what I really wanted. Looks is one thing, and balancing all the other elements involved was a whole other animal, but I was ready to tame it.

CHAPTER 35

The days were moving faster, and even though I wasn't stressing about anything, my mind continued to ponder whether I was fully prepared for what was ahead of me. I felt like I did my time as wisely as I could, but I still had thoughts about whether I could really be fully prepared for the unknown. Me and Gabrielle were speaking more often, and the topic came up of her wanting to see me before I got released.

"I showed your picture to Ashley and Christie."

"Why did you do that? What they say?" I couldn't help but laugh.

"Ashley said you look like you can make a woman fall in love and Christie said you look good."

"I still got some work to do before I get anywhere near satisfied."

"So how far are you away from me now?"

"Like forty-five minutes away. Why?"

"Really that's not far. Send me a visiting form so I can come see you before you get out."

"I'm not sending you another visiting form so you can start acting funny and not come again."

"Brandon, for real, send me one. I have a car now, I'll really come."

I was reluctant to send her the form because of how

things went last time. But I was getting so close to being released, I couldn't allow anything to disrupt my composure. I mailed her the form the next morning and wouldn't bring up the topic again. If she came, then cool, but if not then I would address it once I was out. Our next phone conversation started out light but got deep really quick.

"I sent off that visiting form today," she said.

"Yeah, we'll see."

"What the fuck you mean, we'll see?"

"What I tell you about talking to me like that?" I laughed.

"I'm just sayin' you should be happy. You know I'm lazy."

"You only lazy when it comes to me, not anybody else."

"It's not like that. I don't be goin' to see nobody else in prison. A year or two ago this guy wanted me to come see him, but I couldn't figure it out."

"You were about to go see somebody else and not come see me, huh?"

"I didn't go see him, so I don't feel like that's worth talking about. I want another bracelet. I wear the one you got me all the time."

"I'll get you another one when I get out."

"I really want some more charms, and I want to get Aaliyah one too."

"Okay, so how about when I get out, I get you some more charms for yours and we get Aaliyah one too and the both of you can get like matching charms. Sounds like a plan to you?"

"Yeah if I don't have a boyfriend, you can do that."

"What you say?" I twisted my head towards the receiver

to make sure I was actually on the phone and wasn't trippin'.

"I said if I don't have a boyfriend you can do that."

"You not getting' no boyfriend. I'm yo boyfriend."

"No you're not." She laughed.

"I don't know why you gotta keep cheating on me."

"We are not together. You're my best friend." She laughed again.

"I'm not goin' for you being with nobody when I get outta here."

"You know I don't like when you get like this."

"I want my spot back, Gabrielle."

"What spot? You never had a spot." She laughed.

"I'm serious you can play coy all you want. I want my spot back, and whatever I gotta do to get it will be done."

"How did we get here?"

"I don't know if you think it's just because I'm in jail that I feel this way and when I get out I'm going to change, but I assure you that I won't."

"It just seems wrong from the circumstances of how we know each other. And you know how William is—I don't want him to take it out on David. My son loves him, for what reason I don't know."

"He's supposed to love him. That's his father, and that's why I said if I had to, I would wait a few years for us to be together. By that time David would be basically grown and it wouldn't matter what anyone thought."

"I don't want to be sneaking around for us to be together. That's whack, it shouldn't be that way."

"I don't want to be sneakin' around either, but if that's

the sacrifice I have to make for a few years in order for us to be together then I'm willing to do that."

"I don't want you sacrificing years of your life for me. And it's like I get blamed for everything. Aaliyah's dad don't deal with us at all because when I left for a while I let him stay at my apartment, but when my landlord contacted me I had to come back, and I just kicked him out and he's still mad about that because of the money he lost for the rent. He didn't get her nothing for her birthday or graduation. Then William is barely around as it is, and if we're together I know he'll take it out on David and then it'll be my fault."

"None of that is really your fault, Gabrielle. At the end of the day they are going to be around when they want to on their terms, no matter what."

"Then you don't hear the stuff I do from William."

"I'm not about to let anybody put their hands on you or hurt you."

"I don't know. When you were out, we were close but not this close."

"Yeah, it's just throughout the years things progressed into what they are now. I genuinely love you, Gabrielle. I'm all for you. You have done a lot of things to hurt me, but I believe you push me away because you're scared of the unknown. You be having me heated, but I know I could never hurt you. Like I can't make this shit up, I can't picture my life without you, and I just don't want you to let other people to come in between us. We never have a problem when it's just us, only when other people get involved is when we bump heads."

In her soft, sweet voice, she said, "Can we just talk about something else right now?"

"Yeah, of course. I'm yo best friend, you know dat and I know dat. We can figure out the details about everything else later."

"Okay."

I didn't want to press the issue any further. I loved Gabrielle with all I had, but I didn't know if I could handle her being with another man once I was home. While I was away was one thing, but I figured she wouldn't need another man because I was going to provide for her all she could ever want or need. Our next phone conversation was kind of tense. I only called to tell her I loved her and that I would talk to her later, but she snapped at me.

"You should appreciate that I call you and tell you that I love you."

"You always tryna get you a sneak in."

"Always tryna get me a sneak in?"

"Yeah, talkin' about you just called to tell me you love me. I'ma look you in yo eyes and tell you, so I hope you prepared."

"You gone look me in my eyes and tell me what?"

"That I love you as a friend. That we're friends to the end." She said it in a light manner with a deep undertone to it, and I didn't like that at all. I felt the familiar piercing blow to my heart, but I hid it well.

"Whatever, Gabrielle."

"See this is what I'm sayin, it's like you don't listen to nothin' I say, just blow me off and say whatever, and that's not fair."

"Because I don't believe that, Gabrielle."

"Okay, well you said you only called for that, right? I been on the phone with people all day, and I'm irritated and I just want to lay down because I know tomorrow is going to be worse at work."

"Alright."

"Okay, love you too."

I knew I was soft on her and understood that I could be viewed as sentimental at times. Maybe I took her comment too deep. My energy was off when I called her, and I was a little down. Plus I could tell that she was having a bad day as well, so maybe that was why she snapped at me. I decided that I wouldn't call for a few days. Her birthday was coming up, and after she asked me what I was going to get her, even though I knew I couldn't get her the $475 designer bag she wanted, I agreed that I would send her half the money for her birthday. I wanted to focus on my release and didn't want any tension between us so I left the issue of us being together alone. Also I knew that she would be accepted as a visitor soon, and we would have the chance to see each other again after seven years of being separated. I knew that on this visit, a lot would be said and understood. We both would have the chance to see if the feelings we said we had for each other would ignite and blossom or deter and remain stagnant. Either way, it would be a moment of truth.

CHAPTER 36

I never watched a lot of television, even in prison. Nothing could really hold my attention. Every now and then I could catch a good series that was worth watching for entertainment purposes, but other than that television was another waste of time. If it wasn't a show about real estate, the stock market, or the news, it was a distraction. I liked to fill my mind with things that I could apply toward my success. *Shark Tank* was one of my favorite shows. I was intrigued by the way entrepreneurs present their companies to the sharks and listened to the jargon they used as they publicly and effortlessly crunched numbers and discussed the dynamics of the potential contracts.

About a year ago, someone suggested that I watch a movie called *The Notebook*. But when the movie came on, I only watched five minutes and inadvertently transitioned into doing something else. This day as I was channel surfing, I rolled right into it. For some reason, after all the other times that I had overlooked it, something compelled me to watch it. As the story unfolded it showed me just how deep love could really be, and that no matter what, if it was real, nothing could come in between it. The two main characters, Noah and Allie, met at a carnival, but their attraction was organic. Even though they only spent one summer together, in those few short months sprouted a love that would last for the remainder of their lives. They seemed to argue a lot and could never really agree on anything, but at the end of the day they were crazy about each other and how they felt overpowered everything else. Noah met Allie's parents, who were extremely wealthy, and her mother felt Noah wasn't good enough for her daughter. The summer was coming to an end, and right after Allie and Noah had a fight, she had to leave and go back home. They didn't get to see each other before she left, but Noah wrote her one letter a day for a whole year. Allie's mom intercepted each letter and kept them from her. Years later, Noah saw Allie walking down the street as he was riding the bus. He asked the driver to stop multiple times, but he wouldn't so Noah just jumped off the bus. By the time he had made it to her destination, which was a restaurant, he realized that her fiancé was waiting for her.

Noah didn't make contact but went back home to the house he had just purchased. The summer they met he told Allie he would buy this same house and fix it up, and once Allie added her input, she made him promise to make the house to her liking. Noah felt that if he created the house the exact way she asked him to, that somehow Allie would come back to him.

Years passed and Allie was soon to be a married woman, but at her dress rehearsal she saw Noah's picture in the newspaper and returned to the house and realized that he made it exactly like she described all those years ago. Once they talked and made up, there was no denying that they still loved each other, but Allie was engaged. Once that concept came up, they began to fight because Allie didn't know what to do. As fate would have it, Allie left her fiancé and chose to be with Noah, and after a visit from her mother she finally received all the letters Noah wrote to her all those years ago. As they grew old together, Allie developed Alzheimer's disease. Before it took her mind over completely, she gave Noah a notebook that she had that held all of the details of how they met, their separation, and how they reunited. She told him, "Soon this disease is going to take over and I won't remember anything. But read this to me, and no matter where I am, I'll come back to you." Once her condition got worse, he would sit with her and read the story. Most of the time she wouldn't remember a thing but would always say she liked the story. There were a few times that her memory would completely come back and they would enjoy their love again, but through it all, even until death, he never left her side.

After I saw the movie I was in shock. I felt like I was in the same situation and would never give up the love between me and Gabrielle. Something compelled me to share the story about the movie I just saw with Gabrielle, so I wrote her a letter expressing what I saw in the film.

The next time I called, she thanked me for the money I sent for her birthday and brought me up to speed about how William came around and gave David and Aaliyah some money. Then the conversation took a turn.

"That's why I think we wouldn't work. I want to keep things cordial with William for the sake of David, and if we're together then it's gonna be drama."

"I don't get it, so what do you think will happen if you tell him that I'm your best friend?"

"I'll never tell him that, he'll trip."

"That's what I'm sayin'. So what's the difference if we're secretly best friends or secretly together?"

Prior to this conversation, Gabrielle told me her ex-boyfriend was trying to get back with her, and after that I sent her a message stating that if she let another man come in between us again, I was going to leave her.

"Why did you send me that message?"

"What do you mean?"

"The part about you leaving if I let someone come in between us. I thought that was rude."

"I was just letting you know where I stood. What's the point of lettin' someone else in yo life when you know I'm about to come home?"

"This has been goin' on wit us a long time now, and I should have been stronger. I don't know if I just said things because they sounded good at the time, but this is gonna be too much."

"So basically you tellin' me that all the things you told me wasn't true? That you been lying to me for years about lovin' me and wantin' to be with me?"

"No, Brandon, it's not like that."

"You saying that yo word don't mean shit."

"Brandon, don't be like that. I just put shit outta my mind sometimes because of all the things I've been through in my life. You know how hectic my life is."

"Don't be like what? All of a sudden since somebody wants to come around and be nice to you part-time, you ready to turn on me? You always leavin' me hangin' and turnin' yo back on me, and every time you bring yo ass back, I embrace you and love you like you never left. You been all around the fucking world and you haven't come to see me once."

She paused. "Why didn't you say somethin'?"

"What the fuck you mean why I didn't say somethin'? I shouldn't have to say shit. You don't ever have to say shit when it comes to me. When you need me or are in trouble, I'm there even when you don't ask."

"I feel you should have been said somethin' instead of holdin' all this in. You should have told me that you needed me to come visit you, that's fake."

"No that's not fake, you fake, and you don't give a fuck about me."

"I hate you, Brandon." She hung up.

I didn't mean to go so hard on her, but it was like she was oblivious to all the things she put me through. My emotions just took over. When I called back, she didn't answer. I called again and she picked up.

"We have to talk if we gon' solve our issues, Gabrielle."

"I hate you, Brandon. You making it like I don't care about you, and that's not right."

"I'm just goin' off yo actions."

"You can save all this for when I come to see you, because I know that's why you want me to come. You got me over here crying thinkin' about what you said."

"I was upset. I dropped a tear or two myself sayin' what I said."

"For real?"

"Yeah."

"You be emotional."

"I think it's just my passion for you and our relationship."

"Most of the time when we talk, you be like that."

"No I don't. I think I'm mostly like that when you mention another man pursuing you."

"You are territorial."

"I'm probably a little possessive too."

She laughed. "You are, that's why no man is going to allow me to have you as my best friend. You extra."

"It's really because they wouldn't have your best interests at heart."

"Shut up, you wouldn't let me have a male best friend if I was wit you."

"I would if you told me about him in the beginning. If I love you I have to accept what comes with you. Everyone comes with some form of baggage, it's just for us to determine what we will or won't accept. Either way, people are going to have to accept me."

"I don't have to tell nobody about you."

I laughed then said, "You right, you don't. Because no matter what man is in your life or tries to come along, I'ma outdo all of 'um anyway. So you're right, they would never accept me."

It was crazy how the conversation went from us being frustrated with each other, then angry, to both of us shedding tears, to us laughing and being happy. Throughout all my life no woman has never had this much power over me. Even though she had done me wrong and left me a few times I still trusted her, and wanted her to feel my love at all cost. I just couldn't have her turning on me for another man when I knew she loved me and we belonged together. I wouldn't allow it. If she turned on me again, even though it would be the hardest thing I had to do, I would remove myself from her life until she understood that I wasn't accepting second place to no man.

CHAPTER 37

"Brandon, what you on, man? We short a man and could use some good defense on the court."

"I'll run a game, just let me read the bulletin board real quick," I answered. There was a memo posted by the board that said, "As of July 1st, all applicants must send in a copy of their driver's license or state ID with their application or the applicant's visiting form will be denied."

Damn, Gabrielle probably didn't do that, I thought. *The rules had been the same so long that I never had to keep up with them. I can't blame her for not being able to come visit now because it's my fault for us not being able to see each other.* The next time we spoke, I could sense she was bothered by something.

"Hey, my queen. Whatchyo fine ass doin'?"

"Ooohhh talk that talk to me."

"How you doin'?"

She sighed. "I'm okay."

"What's wrong, baby?"

"I just have so much on my plate right now. I'm not really prepared to move, and my lease is up next month. I still haven't been able to get the kids stuff for school and . . ." She was talking fast, and I could feel the pressure on her.

"Gabrielle, calm down. It's gone be okay."

All of a sudden, I could hear her crying and sniffling. "I'm just so overwhelmed right now with everything."

"Don't stress yourself out, Gabrielle. I know you have a lot on your plate right now, but you have to stay focused and stay balanced."

"I just need some time to think to myself."

We ended the call. To hear her like that broke my heart. I knew she needed me, but I felt helpless. I had just sent her some money for her birthday and really didn't have a lot of cash left—only a few hundred so I could get a few items that I needed once I was released. But I couldn't sit back and let her struggle if I could help. I emailed her and broke down the scenario about how much money I had left in my account and that I was sending her half. We spoke two days later.

"I don't want you to send me that money."

"What do you mean? Why not?"

"You're going to need stuff when you get out, and I don't want you struggling tryna help me."

"Look, I'ma send it anyway, I'ma be okay when I get outta here. It's not like I'm goin' home. I'll still be in a halfway house for a while, so it's not like I need a wardrobe or anything. I just need a few items and I'm cool."

"Brandon, you need to take care of yourself."

"Taking care of you is me taking care of myself."

"I don't want you to, but if you do, I'll just get you some stuff for when you get out."

The money was already on its way. I didn't care what she was talking about. If she needed me, I would support her at all cost. We had a brief conversation after she got the money.

"Why did you do that? You so irritating." Then she laughed.

"Why I do what?"

"Send me that money. That means you sent it before we even spoke. You just knew I needed it, huh?"

"I sent it after the conversation we had when you were having your meltdown. I can't sit back and allow you to feel that way or go through situations on your own if I can do something about it."

"Thank you. I'm about to go look at this place to see how it is. I gotta get this in order."

"Handle your business, and I'll get at you later."

"Okay, I love you."

My mind went to my release. Time was going by quick, and I knew I would be out there to be with Gabrielle and better support her and the kids soon.

I had recently been informed about a Facebook conversation that I was the topic of by some people from my old circle. Certain individuals felt that I was tripping for the position I was taking when it came to me not dealing with them. They felt my situation had nothing to do with them, so I couldn't be mad that no one came through for me, and that the time I did had messed my mind up. Initially, I couldn't believe the audacity of the people making these statements. Then I switched my lens. I understood that by severing ties, there would be some resentment towards me. They wanted me to be who I once was, giving loyalty blindly to those who didn't deserve it, accepting their counterproductive behavior, taking their words for significant value when really the words they spoke couldn't pass the marker test that a cashier uses to check for a fake bill at a bank.

I had come too far to allow those types of people to be close to me, and above all else I had evolved. My mind had gained so much capacity and insight over the years that I had developed the ability to not only see things but see through them. I always asked the universe to show me exactly what it was that I needed to see in a person or situation for me to come out victorious, so no matter how bad or ugly it was, I wanted to know the truth. In that way I could shape the playing field in my favor. Being observant and paying attention to detail was how I would stay ahead of everyone around me, and being an introvert only enhanced those innate qualities.

People were going to talk about me and have all types of ridiculous stories to tell regardless. Their antics were comical, and I wouldn't allow what was said to affect me in no shape or form. I would just ignore the people who tried to cause controversy in my world. I knew if I ignored them long enough, they would get tired from the lack of attention. I would let my silence speak far better than any words.

CHAPTER 38

It was my birthday, the last one that I would spend locked up, and I was scheduled to leave at the end of the month. I couldn't be happier or more relieved. I had already spoken to my mom and received two birthday emails from family members, but of course the highlight of my day would be when I talked to Gabrielle. I was looking forward to hearing her voice. It would only amplify my mood, but I wasn't prepared for the direction that our phone conversation would take me.

"Hey, my queen."

"Hey, what's today?" I could tell in her voice that she knew.

"I don't know. You tell me what today is."

She started to sing, "Happy birthday to you, happy birthday to you, happy birthday dear Brandon, happy birthday to you."

"Thank you. What you doin'?"

"Nothin' . . ." After a moment of silence, she said, "I have something to tell you."

"Okay, what is it?"

"I don't wanna talk about it today. It's yo birthday, so it can wait until tomorrow."

"No, let's talk about it now."

"I don't wanna mess up your birthday. You sound so happy."

"Gabrielle, we already talked about you bein' honest with me about everything. I don't care if it's my birthday. I wanna know what's goin' on. Is it good or bad?"

"I mean, it's good for me I guess, but bad for you."

I started to feel a fucked-up feeling in the bottom of my stomach. "So what is it?"

She sighed hard. "Well, me and my ex have been talkin' again."

"Talkin' as in the two of you gettin' back together?"

"Yeah, I feel like we didn't get a chance to really make things work."

I paused to gather my thoughts. "Why do you feel this way?"

"Because I had to deal with his child's mother, and I was still doin' me, and we keep coming back to each other. So I think it must be something there."

I couldn't hold in my laughter.

"For real, you just gone laugh at me?"

"Yeah, if that's what you wanna do, go ahead. But this is typical for you, Gabrielle."

"It wouldn't matter if I was with him or somebody else. I don't want to be with you, Brandon."

I paused before I spoke. "You always get to actin' like this when somebody else wants to come around, so I don't believe that. This is the dynamic of our relationship; you keep runnin' off on me and keep gettin' crushed, and then once you broken down, you wanna run back to me so I can put you back together again."

"That's not you puttin' me back togetha, that's you bein' a friend."

"No, that's me puttin' yo ass back togetha again after you leave me hangin' and then they leave you hangin'."

"You don't be listenin' to me, Brandon. I keep tryna tell you, and that's why I keep leavin' because you still be on us being together."

"Gabrielle, you say you don't wanna be wit me and don't love me one minute, but then the next you actin' and talkin' different."

"I just want you to act normal, you be actin' delusional when it comes to us."

I couldn't believe that she just said that to me. "I'm delusional when it comes to our relationship?"

"Yes, you are."

"That's crazy because you make it seem like I just developed these feelings on my own."

"It's only because you're in jail that you're like this." She kept taking shots at the love I had for her.

"Are you serious? Now all of a sudden my feelings aren't real or don't count because I'm in jail. I only go off yo actions and words, and that's why I am the way I am wit you. I don't know. When I fall for someone, I just focus solely on them. I asked you before what my flaws were, and you never told me. Maybe this is one."

"Yeah, it is. I can't even live my life because I feel like I'm turning my back on you."

That broke me. "Why do you feel like you turning yo back on me? Let me tell you somethin', Gabrielle. You don't owe me nothin'. Everything I did for you came from my heart. I was there for you and you were there for me, but we don't owe each other anything."

"But we're like family."

"I get that, but I feel we need to separate because I can't sit back and watch you be with someone else."

"I know he won't let me talk to you if me and him are together."

"I know it's something deeper between us. I love you, Gabrielle. I never meant to be a burden to you."

"You're not a burden."

"This is what it is: you know you love me and wanna be wit me, but you don't wanna deal with the drama it might bring. You'd rather deal with yo ex and the bullshit he comes with even though you know your heart is with me."

"Umm . . . Can I say 'no comment' on that?"

I knew what that meant. "Yeah, you can say that."

"This is why I don't like talking to you. You mess my head up."

"Do you really wanna be wit him?"

"I mean, I guess."

I knew just by her response that she didn't want to be in that relationship. "I will never try to stop you from doing what you wanna do."

"Put to the side you being in love with me. Do you feel like I'm making the right decision?"

"As your best friend, I would still say no, you're not making the right decision. No matter what money they bring to the table, if they're breaking you down mentally and emotionally, you will always end up broken." I gathered the remainder of my thoughts before I spoke again.

"Gabrielle, I love you. You're my best friend, and I don't want it to be like this between us, but I think this is how it has to be."

"You're my best friend too. I love you too. I wear your bracelet every day."

"But that's bullshit, because the only reason you wear it is because he's not around."

She gasped. "I'm just confused."

"I don't want you to be mad at me or think that I don't love you because you know that's not the case."

"I know you love me. This just seems like a fairy tale."

"You won't hear from me for a while."

"I don't have a best friend like you in my life." Then she paused. "I gave you my Facebook page."

The automated voice said, "You have sixty seconds remaining."

Things got silent.

"I love you."

"I love you too."

CHAPTER 39

I couldn't believe the dramatic turn my life just took. I was on top of the world being so close to being released and me and Gabrielle on good terms, but then it all shifted. Gabrielle was my better half, what was I supposed to do without her? Without Gabrielle's love, I knew I would never reach my fullest potential because my energy and passion would never burn like they did for her. I could do all the pretending in the world, but she would forever have my heart no matter what happened. I had to address the things she said and release the remaining thoughts in my mind plus the feelings in my heart. I decided to write her one last email before we separated again.

Good morning Mi Amor,

I just want to touch on a few key components from our conversation yesterday, after that things can be what they are.

The issue with your ex:

I will never be cool with you being with someone else other than me but I'm just looking at his track record that's all. It's a lot of things that you haven't told me when it comes to the relationship between you and him, but I know that's only because it really isn't shit good to say about him. That relationship has stressed you completely out, on top of all the other things that you already have to deal with. You have hidden a lot of things from me and I still accepted what you came to me with and utilized it to assist you in your growth, even though you only gave me very little to work with. If being with him will make you happy then do that, just make sure he treats you like the queen that you are, don't accept anything less.

The disrespect from you towards me:

I've sat behind this wall for years and allowed you to do things that I just wouldn't accept from any other woman on this planet. My enemies have more respect for me than you do sometimes and that's starting to really bother me. You have said some crazy things before but when you said I was delusional when it comes to our relationship, I won't lie I would have never expected you to say something like that to me, but I'm glad I know how you really look at me. That's not even the worst part, to hear you say that my flaw is loving you crushed me. Are you serious, that's my fucking flaw Gabrielle loving you? I know I'm in prison and have been for a long time but you keep throwing that in my face, so now after all these years my love isn't real because I'm in prison? You think just because I'm in here that I would just go through all the things we have been through together? I am fucking in love with you. How many times did you leave me Gabrielle? You just walk in and out of my life when you want to on your terms, and when I'm getting close to your heart you purposely hurt me and leave me to try to pick up the pieces and then come back and do the shit all over again. What man would send a woman money from jail after she told him that she danced for money sometimes, then comes around when she wants to and leave whenever she gets ready? Not none I know, if anything they would have been trying to get money out of you but I never asked for a dime. I took pride in being there for you and the kids. What's

BEAUTIFUL CONSEQUENCES

the sad thing about all this is you told me how people were not keeping their word to you, how everybody just left you hanging so I stepped up to show you that my love was real, and let you know I would never do you like that but then you turn around and do the same shit to me that everybody else was doing to you, don't you see that? I can't forget this, you said you feel like you can't live your life because you feel like you're turning your back on me, I interpret that two ways. You feel like that because you don't want to deal with me like that anymore because now since I'm coming home, you feel no need to pretend anymore about how you feel about me. Or you feel that way because you know deep down your heart is with me and that this is what you want but since you can't figure out how to be with me and manage the drama that may come, you just try to leave but it makes you feel some type of way. If it's the first, then I don't want to be a burden to you anymore. To hear the woman you love more than anything say that she's only with you because she feels obligated and not out of the love she has for you, that's too much for my heart to handle. I can't sit back anymore and allow you to degrade and discredit my feelings because I'm in prison, that's some bullshit and I'm not rocking with you no more on that alone. You would rather hurt me and destroy what we have all because you don't want to acknowledge and accept the fact that you love me and want to be with me. That's why you said this seems like a fairytale because this seems too good to be true. I know you have had men lie to you about all type of things in order to get what they want and switch up on you, but you know that's not the case with me. I would never lie to you, I know you're just living in fear and scared to be with me, and I understand baby really I do but don't act like you don't love me and have deeper feelings for me, when we both know that's a lie. You want to accommodate everybody else and worry about what they think so I'm going to make things easier for you.

The conclusion:

I can't sit back and allow other people to dictate our relationship, I never have before and I won't start now. I gave you my all from in here and I know it didn't mean much to you since I was in prison but I gave all I had. I appreciate you being honest even though I feel some of what you said wasn't true. I want your life to be as good as it can be and if excluding me out of it will make it better, then I'ma do that for you. It's like I don't see this as the end for us even though we are separating again. I believe and know we both love each other and until we both experience how we feel with each other, then we both will experience discomfort in our lives.

The initial feelings we will encounter will be that something is missing, then it will be an emptiness inside both of us, and finally we will both be miserable. After all the things you put me through, I never gave up or lost faith in us, so I won't lose faith now. I'm going to get my life in order, and I'll be waiting for you. I love you so much Gabrielle don't ever think that I don't. I'ma miss you, please take care of yourself and be careful. Take your time with everything you do, don't try to rush anything and make an impulsive move that will compromise the progress you have made and are going to make. You don't have to hide from me so I can't find you because I'm going to remove myself from your life this time. You won't hear from me for a long time and no matter what happens just know that I love you with all my heart. I just can't sit back and watch you be

BEAUTIFUL CONSEQUENCES

with someone else when I know we're supposed to be together, and if I really am delusional when it comes to us then my ignorance will dissolve as the years go by. I have sat back for a long time and watched you be with people knowing it's supposed to be us, and I just can't do that anymore. I really hope you understand, and I can honestly say at 11:28 am as I write this with tears in my eyes, I love you Gabrielle with all my heart and since this is what's best for you, I will go away like you want me to.

The aftershock of everything hit me hard. I started to become really confused mentally and emotionally. Things in life started to get real dark. Was me being in prison clouding my judgment? Since I was in prison it was like nothing I did was considered valuable. Was I really living in a fantasy world, where I could create the life I wanted and have whatever it was I desired? Maybe I wasn't in control of my life like I thought I was and was just like everybody else. Maybe I had lost track of time, while doing time, and didn't have time to adapt to the new society. Maybe that's why it seemed that everyone was turning on me, maybe in all actuality they were being themselves and I was the one not paying attention to the present moment. Gabrielle kept trying to tell me that she didn't love me, but why, no matter what she said, didn't I believe her? Why did I see her leaving as a representation that she did love me and not that I was running her away with my love? Was I really delusional?

I had read a book a few years prior that left a lifelong impression on me. It mentioned how a person could hypnotize themselves with their thoughts. Was that what I did? Was I just in denial and projecting an image on Gabrielle? Maybe all my efforts would have never amounted to anything. What if I had already lost before I started this quest for her love, and by continuing on this path I was just establishing that in this battle I was indeed a loser? With all these questions and no way to figure things out without her clarity, plus fear, discouragement, uncertainty, and doubt consuming me, I didn't know what to do. I was heartbroken, but this time I didn't feel the need to pick up the pieces and put them back together.

At my deepest moment of bewilderment, something happened. A voice began to speak to me, and even though I had never heard this voice before, somehow it seemed familiar. It was my heart, and it had a lot to say.

"I can't believe that you're acting like this. You need to pay attention to what's going on, get focused, and go after her."

"Go after her? She said she don't love me and made it clear that I'm holding her back in life. I'm a burden to her, so why keep putting myself through this when it's obvious she doesn't want me around?"

"Don't take this the wrong way, but you really are delusional. I know you're going through a lot of different emotions with you getting ready to be released, plus all this with Gabrielle, but let me clarify a few things for you. If you think that woman doesn't love you and want to be with you, then you're the one who can't see what's in front of you. Look at everything that's going on. You know that relationship with her ex will not last, just like before. She needs support, and with you not being there, what else can she do? She told you that the relationship with her ex was toxic. If you sit back and allow her to be in that position for too long without your influence, how can you say you love her? You still don't know what he has done to her that has her stressing out so much. We are not leaving her, especially like that."

"What am I supposed to do, keep chasing her?"

"Remember why she's running, Brandon. It has never been because she doesn't love you. It has always been because of fear. Not only is she scared of what people will say and the potential drama, but she's scared of the love you show her. She has never had someone in her life that loves her the way you do, and it terrifies her sometimes to think that maybe it's not real."

"But she keeps saying that I'm only like this because I'm in prison. She doesn't take me serious."

"Because you're looking at it from the wrong perspective. Digest those words and internalize them. What she's really thinking as she says those words to you is that she believes once you're released that you won't feel the same about her and leave her hanging. That is why she keeps pushing you away, because you have her heart, but she still doesn't know if what you say is real. Don't look at you giving your all from behind these walls as not being enough. No matter what you did from in here, it would never have been enough. She has always needed you there, just as much as you needed her. Her needs have never been fully met, and the only man who can fill that void in her life is you. You stimulate her on all levels—mental, emotional, physical, sexual, and spiritual. You weren't there to protect and provide for her like she needed you to, and now after all these years, when the time comes for you to finally prove your love to her, you're going to just give up?"

"It's just so hard dealing with all this. I said the next time she let another man come between us that I would leave her alone. It's like I'm just letting her do whatever and not standing on my word."

"You have got to let your ego go and put your pride to the side. You have to distinguish when to stand on your word and when not to. You already know that in the game of power and love, nothing is set in stone. You have to remain fluid and flexible until you achieve victory. Don't ever doubt your powers, your intellect, your gift, or me. If you don't lose faith and never give up, you will see that love conquers all. Never take things at face value. You have the power to see through things and shape the future how you want it. Whether you know it or not, she'll be waiting to really see if the things you've said to her all these years are true. I promise, once you prove your love to her in the flesh, she will be yours."

I could only blame myself for all this, because I put us in a vulnerable position by confessing how I felt about her without being able to be there to fully support her, which left our relationship susceptible. Just like Noah did for Allie in *The Notebook*, I kept our love alive even when she couldn't remember.

A quote I had written down a few years back came to mind: "Sometimes, the harder you chase that which you most desire, the farther it will run from you. Try to be very still. Be at peace with yourself, be grateful for all you have, all you are. The object of your affections will become curious and will come to you in time."

After reading that astrology book, I had started to read our horoscopes in the paper. One about myself stood out a lot in my current situation: "There's a powerful driving beat behind your love, a rhythm that moves everything forward. Just be careful not to overpower anyone with your energy, because that would be counterproductive to your desire."

I had come to realize that I was a very emotional person, and channeling my emotions correctly would produce great power and success for me. I understood that my and Gabrielle's relationship was a delicate situation, and I couldn't push too hard from my current position. I needed to take a more subtle approach. Of course, I was territorial when it came to her and wanted to come home and be assertive and let guys know that she was off limits, but I knew I couldn't do that right away. I would have to maneuver correctly to overcome the obstacles between us.

I had two options once I got released. If I hadn't heard from her by that time, I could call and see if she would be willing to meet and have a conversation. Option two would be that I wouldn't contact her at all for a while and just let things play out without my influence, expecting the best outcome. I knew just sitting back and watching at a distance wasn't a favorable move. If I weren't involved I would have to accept whatever happened without putting forth a wholehearted effort. If I didn't contact her things would be different, because she wouldn't know where I was.

I wouldn't know what to do until it was time for me to leave prison, so I would wait to make that decision after the last few weeks went by and it was time for me to emerge. Only then would I evaluate everything in its entirety and know what to do.

CHAPTER 40

My mind was in overdrive, and I couldn't settle it for nothing, but it wasn't in the typical fashion. Most of the strong inclinations I was experiencing revolved around challenging and contesting conventional wisdom. A short story from one of my favorite books came to the top of my brain. There was a woman who was in a marriage that was suffering, and even though the woman wanted to work things out, her husband wanted out of the relationship. They ended up getting a divorce, and the man moved on with his life, but she still loved him and wanted to be with him. This woman of faith never entertained the thought that her marriage was over. She continued to live her life as if her husband was still there. When she made dinner, she made a plate for him. She left the side of the closet that he once occupied open and never filled the space. She never slept on his side of the bed. All these actions signified that he was present, even though he wasn't. She continued this behavior for an entire year, until one day he returned, and they remarried and lived happily ever after.

Most people would consider this woman insane for carrying on her life in such a manner when clearly her husband didn't want to move forward in the marriage, but I was beginning to understand that the people who thought this way had no vision, lacked faith, and never experienced a strong enough desire in their hearts to defy the normal standards and produce exceptional results. People said that doing the same thing and expecting different results was the definition of insanity, but that statement irritated me to my core. A lot of people in our history books were once considered insane because they continued to do the same thing and failed while everyone else laughed and criticized them. It was because they had vision and unwavering conviction in their hearts. Malcolm X, Henry Ford, and Isaac Newton all walked down this path and never let anything stop them, and they single-handedly changed the way civilization is today. Most people settled for instant gratification only because they were lazy, had no drive or ambition, and lacked creativity. Those who possessed those qualities never let fear or obstacles or misfortune stop them. If you adopt the mindset that quitting is not an option and that whatever you're striving for has to happen, then the universe will bend to your will.

I knew I had to display this same type of faith and conviction as the woman in the story. If me and Gabrielle weren't speaking after I got released, I would pick furniture with her in mind, I would buy clothing that I believed would look good on her and put it in my closet as if we shared it. On my dresser I would have perfume bottles that would be all hers, as if she was there, with each scent representing the multiple ways she stimulated me. I would buy bodywash and lotion and candles, so when it was time, I could run a bath for her, wash her up, give her a massage and pamper her like she deserved. To top it all off I would buy her the ring I promised her while I was still in prison. If I had to go down this road, it would represent exactly what Noah did when he built the house that Allie said she wanted in order to bring her back. It was the law of attraction in its purest form.

I wouldn't allow myself to get romantically involved with another woman. Noah had someone to try to settle his sexual urges until Allie inevitably returned, but he never gave his heart to another woman. If I had to, I would accept attention from another woman, but my heart belonged to Gabrielle. I would be delicate and patient but wouldn't waste any time in my quest for her love.

CHAPTER 41

Now with under two weeks left, it was starting to settle in that I was actually leaving. I had just took my release photo and all my other affairs in order for me to be transferred. I hadn't spoken to Gabrielle since my birthday, so I decided to call.

"I thought you weren't dealing with me anymore," she said.

"I know what I said, but no matter what we're going through I should never let that stop me from checking on you and the kids."

"Aww, that's so sweet." Then things got quiet. "Are you okay?" I felt like she was playing on my intelligence, even though I heard the sincerity in her voice. Whenever things weren't right between us, life wasn't right for me, but I didn't want to talk about it at the moment.

"I don't really wanna get into it right now."

"I talk to you about everything, even when I don't want to, and that's how you gone act towards me?"

"Now you bluffin'! When you don't wanna talk about somethin', you either try to switch the subject, rush me off the phone, or hang up."

"Do it have something to do with me?"

"I mean I do have a lot on my mind, and you are a major part of what I'm going through right now." Things got silent again. "I miss you, Gabrielle."

"Um hmm."

"You comin' to see me when I get out?"

"Yeah."

"You don't have to say yeah just because. If you not comin' you can say so."

"I told you I'm comin'. I'm about to take a shower. Just call me when you get out."

"Why are you rushin' me off the phone?"

"I'm sayin' you was all quiet earlier, now you wanna act like you got somethin' to say."

"Gabrielle."

"What?"

"Stop treating me like that."

"Just call me when you get out."

"Aight."

A few days passed, and I had a strong inclination about her. I knew I wouldn't be able to properly articulate my words on the phone, so I decided to write her a message.

Good morning sweetheart,

This is what I see:

When I look at you, I see the pressure that you've been under for a long time. I see how you've been struggling to get things in order for you and your children so that you can give them the life that you feel they deserve. I know how you have been manipulated, taken advantage of, lied to and led down a path under false pretenses only to find out that you were being played. I know that you feel unappreciated and undervalued by the men and people in your life, who seem to never care to

BEAUTIFUL CONSEQUENCES

hear you or take your cares and worries into consideration. I see that you have been hurt so many times that you don't know whether or not if someone is actually being genuine and honest with you or if it's just another game to get over on you. With all the heartbreak you've experienced, it has left you completely confused about what is actually right and what isn't, and whether or not what you think is really the right decision or not. I see this extremely strong woman with the qualities that are rare, that only a select few get to see and would make any man proud to have in his woman. Your strength only comes from all your pain, which in retrospect reveals how fragile your heart and emotions really are. You are a delicate creature that really only wants to be loved and protected. You want someone to respect you, to honor your wishes, to see you as an equal and above all else to commit to making your children and you happy. God has blessed both of us to have each other in our lives. When each of us had no one worth the effort of investing our individual time, emotions and thoughts and with all the chaos in our life, you don't know how to deal with the relationship that has blossomed between us. This is what I see when I look at you and I haven't seen you physically in almost eight years, maybe I'm right or maybe I'm wrong. I wonder what I will see once I see you in person. I believe we are in each other's life for a reason and not a season but if I'm wrong, we had a good run and our season lasted almost a decade. I never thought that I would ever have someone like you in my life and I think that's why I feel like I can't let you go. If I'm your best friend or ever was your best friend then I could never be delusional about our relationship, Gabrielle don't disrespect me like that again. I hope you have a good day.

It took me a while to compose that email. I always did my best to be understanding when it came to her and see things from her perspective. I was grateful that she agreed to come see me. I knew that it was easy for a person to camouflage themselves behind phone interactions and emails. But when it came to interacting in person, if you were an analytical person like me, it was a totally different world. You could tell from eye contact, tone of voice, and body language if someone was lying to you and how they were feeling, and you could use that to gain leverage. Even though I knew this was a great strength of mine, I understood that it came at a cost. Sometimes I would overthink things, and I often made certain simple things complicated, which could cost me valuable time.

All of a sudden I started to have a strong thought about my father. Both of my parents would say things to me when I was younger that I really couldn't make any sense of. But now looking back, I realized that they just expected more out of me because they knew my potential. When I used to call people my friends, both scolded me for using that word so loosely. My father would say, "Those same dudes that you runnin' around wit are gone be the same ones pointing you out in court." Or when I would do something that was beneath my nobleness, my mother would say, "Boy, if you had a brain, you'd be dangerous." As a teenage kid I could never grasp what any of these declarations meant, but now it all made perfect sense.

The thing that resonated most with me in the present moment was my father saying, "A person will tell you the truth even when they lie, if you listen hard enough." I knew sometimes Gabrielle would lie to me or say things that she didn't mean to push me away; even though I wanted to believe her words sometimes, something inside me wouldn't allow myself to entertain such statements. Seeing her in person would tell me everything and allow me to see the truth as to whether or not she actually loved me or it was all fake.

Three days later I got an email from her.

I think it's best I don't see you. I am building my family and things are going great. I wish you the best. Good luck with everything?? I changed my number and have moved btw.

In the background I heard, "Brandon . . . Brandon . . . you good?"

"Yeah, I'm good. I just zoned out for a minute. I'm done on here anyway." I had to go to the room and sit on my bunk to process what I read. A wave of confusion and sadness washed over me. She had just given me her word that she was coming to see me, and now she was stating otherwise. My mind started racing. I knew that my release was no longer a secret because the new DOC protocol was to put an offender's release date online, even if it was work release, so word had probably spread that I was on my way out. I figured that William was probably now trying to come around more often and be supportive of her and their son since he found out that I was coming home, in order to block our relationship, and there was no telling what he was saying to Gabrielle to keep us apart. It was great for David to have his father in his life, but it bothered me that someone would influence her to turn on me. I started to feel like I was losing her. I was about to write a response out of anger, but I knew that wouldn't be right. Still, I had to express myself. I decided to send her one last message including the name of the halfway house and the address.

This is where I'll be. I don't like when you do things like this, I just wanted to see you . . . I'm always there for you when you need me.

I was devastated, but I knew I had to get a better perspective on the situation. If I came out with this negative energy after all this time of being locked away, it could ruin everything I had built and was about to create. I had to remember that the Most High and the Universe had never let me down before, so I had to exhibit faith in the face of doubt and be strong until she returned.

CHAPTER 42

The day of my release had finally arrived. The night before I didn't get any sleep, but that wasn't out of the ordinary. I got up earlier than usual just to make sure I was completely ready and so I could speak to a few people before I left. Me and Mr. Washington shared a few laughs. I appreciated all the words of wisdom and encouragement that he offered me for the past few months. I planned on keeping in contact with him, to assist him in any way I could once he was out. I exercised for a short circuit and I was ready to go. In the holding tank, it was only me and one other person.

"Man, it looks like it's only us leaving today. I can't wait until I get to the halfway house so I can order some real food. I'm craving a Big Mac and a twenty-piece chicken nugget, a large fry, and a large vanilla milkshake."

"I never really thought about what I would eat once I got out. I know I wanna try some different types of food but stay away from the majority of things that don't serve the body well."

"I hear you, man, but me, I'm eating whatever I can get my hands on. They had us in here eating God-knows-what for all this time. I gotta make up for lost time." He burst out laughing.

We heard a key insert into the cell door, and it opened.

"Reid."

"Yeah."

"Come sign your release papers."

We walked down the hall to a window where a female guard was sitting. "How are you doing today, sweetheart?" she asked.

"I really don't know what to say. This really doesn't even seem real right now."

"I understand what you mean. Just sign your name on the lines with the X on it, and you'll be all good to go."

I started thinking back to all those years ago when I was sitting in a holding cell in the county jail, waiting to see what was going to happen. Until that one day the CO came around with a breakfast tray and slid my charge papers under the door. At that point, I didn't know if I would ever see the other side of the wall again. And now I was signing my release papers.

"Thank you."

"You're welcome."

On the ride to the halfway house my mind was all over the place, and since I didn't get any sleep the night before I was tired, but I forced myself to stay awake for the ride. With all the thoughts going through my mind, the most prominent thought I had was about Gabrielle. We hadn't spoken since that last message, and I realized that I didn't check my emails before I left but figured she wouldn't send anything anyway. This was the moment we both had been anticipating for years, and now that it had come, we weren't even speaking.

I arrived at the halfway house and got settled in. I

wouldn't be able to leave until the following week, so I had to get acquainted with my surroundings. The very first night was hectic for me. I developed an intense headache. I tried my best to stay calm and relax, but it seemed like it continued to get worse. I could barely lay down or be still, so I went to a window to try and get some fresh air to breathe and feel a breeze on my head. This lasted for almost two hours, and then it finally subsided. I didn't have an explanation for what could have caused it, so I just thought it was a phase and for the rest of the night I was okay. Yet the following night, the pain came back more intense than before. I felt sharp, deep pains in the middle of my brain starting from my temple. I didn't know if I was just in shock or if it was something actually wrong that I should go get checked out. Once again, after a few hours the pain went away, but this continued for a week straight every night, and the last two days the pain lasted for a straight forty-eight hours. The staff called an ambulance, and I was sent to the hospital. I couldn't believe that nine days after being released I was sitting in a hospital with an ice pack on my head. The doctors said they believed that I was having migraines, and after they did a CT scan, they affirmed that there was nothing to worry about. They gave me a cycle of pills to take my blood pressure down.

"We're going to give you a shot to stop the pain. After a while, you're going to feel drowsy, but we're going to leave you in this room in the dark for a few hours before we release you."

I felt lost. I wanted badly to call Gabrielle but decided not to. What would I say anyway? "Hey, I love you, I'm in the hospital"? It just wouldn't look right, even though I felt she should be there for me no matter what.

Leaving the hospital was a tad bit difficult. I didn't have a ride and no one to call that could come get me. *I know I'm not too far from the halfway house, but I'm not too familiar with downtown to navigate my way from here, especially feeling the way I do off whatever they shot me with.* I thought. *I'ma just have to take a cab since I don't have any other options.*

"Excuse me, sir, do you know where nineteenth and Nicollet is?

"Sure, that's not too far from here."

"Thank you." The ride back was a blur, and it seemed like I was only in the cab for about five minutes.

"Here we are."

"How much do I owe you, sir?"

"Eight fifty."

Luckily I had some cash on me to pay the fare. "Here you go. You can keep the change."

"Thank you, you have a good night."

I made my way through the doors with my hospital papers in hand, and as soon as I got upstairs to my room, I passed out.

CHAPTER 43

I slept the whole next day after coming back from the hospital. When I finally did get up and started moving around, I felt rejuvenated. I got my affairs in order for work the following day and just let the day play out. Steve was the first person to come see me once I got released. He gave me his word that once I came home, he would assist me in any way possible. Steve was just learning how to walk again because he was recovering from having six strokes, but he didn't let that stop him. He was still walking and driving even though he was half paralyzed. We had made arrangements to link up that weekend on my first pass so we could talk and get some things understood. That morning I walked to Steve's house, and after making sure everything was good, we hopped in his brand-new Camaro and took off.

The first stop was a beauty academy school so I could get a haircut. I knew that more than likely I wouldn't come out with a haircut to my liking, but figured after doing almost eight years and having dudes basically practice cutting my hair, why not let a woman practice on my head. I didn't like the haircut, but the experience was good enough for me, so I tipped the stylist and we left. Our next stop was to a Target so I could get a few things that I needed. On the way there, I enlightened Steve on my relationship with Gabrielle. I knew I could trust Steve with this delicate information, and he wouldn't say anything to anybody.

As I was going through how I felt, I realized that I was having an emotional breakdown. My mood switched, and my energy got really low. Things just didn't seem promising as they once did.

"I understand that you're hurt, but that's because you love hard. And from the way you described everything to me, I know you really care about her and value the relationship between the two of you. I'ma be honest wit you, Brandon. You just got released from doing almost eight years. You don't have any drug habits, no children to take care of, and you don't owe nobody, but you really aren't ready to take care of her like you want to. You haven't got all your affairs in order yet. You need to take your time and handle all the business that will get you in position so you can provide for her. Then you have to understand that you don't know what all she's going through or has been going through. I don't know why you walking around here wit yo head down because you good. Everything will work itself out, just do what you need to do in the meantime. One day the two of you will sit down and talk and then the both of you will be able to figure everything out."

"Yeah, you right."

I did what I could to cheer up temporarily. I had a meeting set up with someone who sent word through a third party that he wanted to see me. B was older than me and had been operating in Minnesota on a major level for a long time. Him and me had never done any business prior to me being sent away, but the respect between us was always there, so when I heard he wanted to meet, I accepted the offer.

"You finally walked that shit down, huh?" he said as we embraced.

"Hell yeah, man. I'm glad that shit is over."

"I don't have no money on me right now, but here go somethin'."

"I appreciate it. What's going on doe?"

He brought me up to speed on what was going on in the streets and a few people that we both knew.

"Yeah, William and nem around here hot as a firecracker."

"What chu mean?"

"Man, they done been caught up wit some guns a few times, from what I hear."

"I don't get why he's ridin' around wit some guns for anyway."

"He basically gang bangin' if you ask me, how you supposed to be where we from and you around here doin' all this shit you got goin' on."

I had to get back to the halfway house before it was too late. We swapped numbers and embraced again. Before B left, he said, "Don't just jump straight out here. If you wanna get right, call me and I'll getchu straight. What everybody else got goin' on don't concern you. Focus on you, get you some females, lay low, and stay out the way."

CHAPTER 44

I had come to the realization that I wasn't happy. After years locked away, anyone else would be joyful to finally be free, but it was the opposite for me. This was not how I had envisioned me coming home. My energy was low and stagnant, and it was like nothing could cheer me up. My focus was lacking, and even with me now having access to so much after being forced to accept so little for so long, nothing seemed interesting. I knew I was blessed to come out of the situation I was just in with my mind still operating at the level that it was and still growing, but I felt like a loser. In a strange way, I felt like I was still in captivity. I was becoming overwhelmed with everything instead of embracing the challenge like I usually did. I was starting to feel like I did when I was locked away, like I was just existing and wasn't really living. How could I when my heart was gone? I didn't want to throw away all the years me and Gabrielle had invested with each other or give up on our relationship, but I didn't know how we could solve anything or move forward if we didn't have a face-to-face conversation. I didn't want to be around anyone, and I didn't care about anything. I was beginning to feel numb, like nothing mattered at all. Most people would turn to drugs or alcohol to numb the pain, but I was developing that feeling naturally. Exercise always relieved me, and even though they barely had any equipment at the halfway house, I still worked out for an hour, five days a week. But even that wasn't even helping like it once did.

My mind went back to a book I had read before being released titled *The Wisest One in the Room*. It said that when a person believes in something, they act in ways that make the belief true, and it prevents them from encountering evidence that it is not. Most people develop a naïve realism that gives them the impression that they see things the way they are and not colored to their expectations and preferences. I wondered if those thoughts were a clear depiction of what I had gone through with Gabrielle. A lot of what I felt our relationship was based on came from Gabrielle and her thoughts in addition to mine, but maybe I had fallen in love with a side of her that only rarely surfaced due to all she had endured over the years? Either way, without us talking and her giving me clarity, I would always feel truly lost.

CHAPTER 45

I had been out for a little over a month now, and even though things were not how I wanted them to be, I knew that no matter what happened I had to continue to have faith and trust the process. I had thought that as soon as I got out, everything I desired would just automatically come exactly how I wanted it to. But things worth having rarely ever came instantaneously. I wasn't in contact with a lot of people, even though word had spread that I was out. Me and Smooth did talk often, but I didn't reach out to him as soon as I got out. Even though Smooth didn't know how deep the relationship was between me and Gabrielle, he knew if anybody had talked to me since I got released it was her, and he sent her a message on Facebook asking if she had talked to me. After I finally contacted him and we caught up, he let me know that he messaged her asking about me.

"Yeah, I haven't talked to her yet. She probably didn't respond to your message either, huh?"

"As a matter of fact, she didn't."

"Me and her both just got a lot goin' on right now, and we tryna figure it out. If she contacts you about me, just let me know what she said before you respond."

"You know I got you. But what's goin' on, bro, why you and her not talking?"

I really hadn't told anyone from my former circle about my relationship with Gabrielle in its entirety. Steve was the only one who knew, and other people just knew she was my best friend. I knew that at the end of the day Smooth was a person I could trust, and I felt what I told him he would keep between us until me and Gabrielle could sort things out.

"My mind and heart have been made up for years. I wanna marry that woman. No matter how it looks or how anyone feels, I love her with all my heart, and I'm not about to let nobody come in between me and her."

"Of course not, bro. Even though, I will say, it's so many women out here for you to choose from if this don't work out."

"Yeah, but none of these females would never mean the same to me or have the value in my eyes that she does. I still need to take my time so I can put myself in position to be the man I want to be in her life and be able to take care of her and the kids. I'm behind financially because I just got out, and I know I can't compete wit these dudes out here in that department."

"Like you said, bro, just take yo time. If you love her like that, then don't give up. You and her came this far. It's all up to you what's gone happen."

A few days went by, and I tried to focus on other things. A philosophy popped in my head, saying, "When you think nothing is happening, that's when everything is happening. And when you think everything is happening, that's when nothing is happening." I knew that I wasn't supposed to take things I saw at face value. I hated being separated from Gabrielle, but I had to have faith that it was only temporary. Then I got a text message from Smooth saying that Gabrielle asked for my number. After I thought about it—even though really there was nothing to think about—I told him to give it to her.

I was only allowed to have my phone during certain hours throughout the day, mainly when I left the halfway house. Almost a week had gone by with no word from her, but one morning while I was at work my phone rang. I didn't recognize the number, but I knew only a few people had my direct phone number, so I answered.

"Hello."

"Hello." It was her.

I slowly got up from my workstation and made my way to the bathroom so we could talk. "How are the kids doin'?"

"They're good."

"What's wrong wit you?"

"What do you mean?"

"You know what I mean."

"I'm just tryna figure out my situation."

"Are you talkin' about with that one guy?"

"Yeah. I didn't call you because my phone is on his plan. This is my mom's phone. I know I don't wanna be wit him anymore. I'm just tryna be done with everything."

We talked for a little while longer and then I went back to work.

My phone buzzed. I had a text message from her. *I miss you.*

Me being a sucker for her, I responded, *I miss you too, things are hard without you.*

I'm sorry for not being there for you and I'm just trying to figure things out.

I understand that, but you can only make so many excuses.

We spoke a few more times that day, and I felt good that we had finally spoken after what felt like forever. I was relieved that at least I knew what was going on. Now I just had to be patient until the time finally came for us to see each other.

CHAPTER 46

A few days had passed, and I hadn't heard anything from Gabrielle. Of course, I wanted to talk to her as much as possible, but I knew I had to wait until she contacted me. As soon as I was getting off work, my phone rang.

"Hey, what are you doin'?" she asked.

"About to get off work, what about chu?"

"Nothin' really. You can't be callin' this phone or textin' it back. I'm just sayin' he can go through all dis shit until I give him all his stuff and get my own phone."

"Gabrielle, I understand."

"So you about to go back to the place?"

"Yeah, but I have a dentist appointment, and after that I'ma just be out until I have to go back at nine o' clock."

"Okay, um . . . I don't have any plans until later. Who's comin' to get you from the dentist?"

"Right now I don't know. What . . . you wanna come get me?"

"Yeah, I'll come. I'ma just get the kids, get dressed, and I'll be there. What time do you think you'll be done?"

"I don't know, maybe an hour or two."

"That should give me enough time."

"Gabrielle, don't tell me you comin' if you not."

"Brandon, I'm serious. I'ma call you in a little over an hour."

"If you don't come, we gone have a serious problem."

"Okay, Brandon."

For this to be coming together out of thin air was raising my awareness level. I knew I wasn't in control of the situation. It was all on her if we were going to see each other or not.

When I got out of the dentist, I saw I had a missed call.

"Hey, I'ma be a little late."

"Whatchu mean, a little late?"

"You know me, I got to procrastinating and moving slow and—"

"See this is the shit I'm talkin' about. You always got an excuse when it comes time to follow through on somethin' for me."

"Brandon, I'm not sayin' I'm not comin'. I'm just sayin' I'ma be ten minutes late, that's all. Have some understanding."

"Have some understanding, are you serious? You do this shit constantly when it comes to me. How much fucking understanding am I supposed to have, Gabrielle?"

"I know you wanna go hard on me, and I know I deserve it, but can it wait until I get there. Brandon, this is our first time seeing each other in a long time. You should be nice to me, not cursing me out."

"Yeah, I guess so. I'll see you when you get here."

I went to the nearby Walmart to wait for her. I was nervous to see her. Pictures could never compensate for having the person you desire right next to you. Then I wondered if she would look different in person than in the pictures, but I knew that no matter how she looked, my feelings would be the same.

"I'm getting ready to pull in the front."

"Alright, what kinda car you in?"

"A blue Nissan."

I walked out the front doors and saw her car, walked to the passenger-side door, and got in. I took my jacket off and put it on the back seat. She looked me up and down, and then we locked eyes. For a moment it was like everything in life stood still, and then she said "hey" with a smile, and I couldn't help but smile as well. "What's up, stranger?"

I couldn't stay mad at her. She pulled up to a nearby restaurant and parked. She had on a cream-colored button-down sweater, but she had it open enough to show that she had on a bedazzled bra. After she parked the car, she looked over at me and we both reached out to hug each other. After we embraced, I couldn't help it, so I started kissing all over her.

In between giggles, she said, "Best . . . friend . . . get back in yo seat . . . you all over me." I wasn't trying to hear that. I went for her bra. In a playful voice, she said, "Brandon, what are you doin', it's people around."

"I don't care, I wanna suck on yo titties."

Then she sat back in her seat so I could do what I wanted. I lifted her bra and started my process. I began licking and sucking on her nipple. The whole time she was watching my every move. "You act like you know how to work yo tongue or somethin'."

As I was licking her nipple, I paused and said, "Do I?"

And all she could say was, "Yeah, you do." So I continued for a little while longer. "You gotta stop, Brandon, it's people comin' out the restaurant. Lift yo shirt up."

I did as she asked and leaned back in the seat. She reached over and started rubbing on my chest and began gliding her hand down to my stomach. I put my hand over hers and guided it down to my dick. As she felt it through my pants, she said, "Let me feel it for real." I unbuckled my belt and pulled my pants down enough to show my hard dick through my boxers. She pulled it out and then massaged for it a while, and with a smile, she said, "Okay, you can put him away now."

After we both got ourselves composed, we went into the restaurant. I held both doors for her as we entered. We sat down and ordered food. Before we started, I grabbed both of her hands and said a silent prayer over our food, and then we began eating. She brought me up to speed on all the events in her life, showed me pictures and videos of the kids and pictures of her, and told me about the drama between her and the guy she was still involved with. As she was talking, I noticed a ring on her finger. This was one of those key things that I was adamantly against when it came to her. I understood that, since I was away, I had to deal with someone potentially coming along and showing interest in her that could jeopardize our connection. I accepted that when I revealed how I felt about her years ago, but rings, tattoos, and babies I just couldn't accept. I couldn't continue to love her to the degree that I did with elements of that nature in the equation. Yet my prior thoughts and convictions would be tested soon, and my definition of unconditional love would be forever transformed.

"Let me see your hand real quick," I said as I held my hand in the air waiting to receive hers.

"Why you wanna to see my hand?" She put her hand inside of mine.

As I began to examine the ring on her finger, my first thought was to take it off because I felt that no man was good enough for her or should have the privilege of thinking he had the right to have her. *This dude really think she belong to him*, I thought. *I'm not about to allow this shit to go on much longer. Once I get my affairs in order, he gotta move around.* As I stared into her eyes, I told her, "I'll get you a better one."

Right after I said that she lifted her other arm, pulled back her sleeve, and said, "See, I told you. I wear your bracelet every day."

I had never seen the bracelet before, so I gently grabbed her wrist to look at it. The charm said "best friends" on it. We finished eating and we left the restaurant. As we were riding back toward the area that the halfway house was in, the conversation got deep.

"Gabrielle, what are we doin'?"

"What do you mean?"

"I mean I'm home now, so I'm tryna figure out what's goin' on wit us."

"Brandon, I just don't know right now. My life is hectic. I've been off and on with this dude for like two years now, and I know it's not the best relationship for me. Then Aaliyah's dad hasn't seen her in a long time because he's mad at me. William is only there for David when he chooses to, so it's like I'm barely getting any help from anybody. Then you, I just keep coming back to you, and I know you're like *what the fuck* when it comes to me, but Brandon, I'm torn. William's family already doesn't like me, and us being together would make them hate me. I know what's between us is real, but I just don't want you to pressure me. I want to have a clear mind so when I make the decision about us, I will be strong, and our relationship will be strong too. Your love is so deep, and I've never had that before, so it does scare me, Brandon."

"Do you think I'm going to hurt you, Gabrielle? You know I would never do anything to hurt you."

"I know. It's just a lot with our past, and I still be thinking about what people will have to say even though it shouldn't matter."

"I can't say I love you and not understand your perspective. You mean so much to me that it's like I can't let you go. I just hate when you put another man before me or let somebody come in between us. I know right now I can't provide for you and the kids like I want and need to, and that's probably why you still dealing with these other guys. But soon I'ma change that. I won't pressure you, but I know my feelings are not going to change. I'm here if you need me, and I won't try to bring no extra drama into yo life while you figure things out."

We talked for a while longer until I had to go back in, but before I got out of the car she said, "Give me a kiss."

I was startled. "What?"

BEAUTIFUL CONSEQUENCES

"You heard me, I said give me a kiss before you leave me, Brandon."

Looking into each other's eyes, we leaned in, and as our lips touched for the first time and our tongues danced, you would have never believed that this was something new for us. I would have never been able to picture what this would be like without experiencing it. It was deep, long, and passionate.

"Now hurry up before you be late." We hugged, and I headed in for the night.

CHAPTER 47

For the next few days, Gabrielle and I talked consistently about my job, how I felt about being released, how she and the kids were doing, and just life in general. For my first ninety days, I would be basically working for prison wages, even though I was back into society. Due to the conditions of the program, I was making three dollars an hour, and half of that went to the halfway house for room and board. I couldn't understand how the ones in control of this system could express that they wanted to assist the people coming out of prison but at the same time set them up for failure. I guess that was the trade-off, though. If you decided to not indulge in this program, then you would still be waiting in prison to be released.

I started to understand that the system was only set up to continuously enslave people. The more people they had behind bars, the more money they could acquire due to the broken families, the loss of hope, the lack of knowledge and finances, not to mention the mental abuse due to the conditions of prison. Nothing about the "Department of Corrections" was about correction or rehabilitation. It was all a business, and it was all up to you to correct yourself and put your life on the right track. I had seen some of the best go through prison and seen how it broke men to the point that they didn't even know themselves anymore.

I prided myself on not allowing what I went through to break me. All the energies attempting to compromise my drive would be eliminated ASAP. Gabrielle was talking about how she had to take care of a few things, and of course I offered to give her some money if she needed it. We agreed that she would come to my job on my lunch break to get the money. My phone buzzed. *I'm outside.*

I went outside like I was having a smoke break and got in the car. "You're not even twenty minutes away from my house," she said.

"So the drive was okay?" As I asked my question, I handed her the money.

"Yeah, this isn't nowhere, and it was easy to get here. How long do you have to work here before you can get a real job?"

"Ninety days. I can start setting up interviews in a few weeks. I look forward to seeing some real money."

Things got quiet for a minute, and we both looked at each other; then we hugged and kissed. I was curious to know what she felt like, so I went to get inside her pants.

"Brandon, stop. I haven't even shaved."

"What does that have to do with anything?"

"I don't want you touchin' me down there until I'm shaved."

"Okay. What you got planned for today?"

"I'ma just go back to the house and take a nap before I go get the kids. What about chu?"

"I'ma finish up here, head back to the place, and just enjoy the bus ride back."

"You know how to ride the bus?"

"A little bit. It's time for me to go back in here. I'll call or text you later."

"Okay, thank you again."

After a few hours, my day was pretty much over. I was grateful for the ride back to the halfway house even though it was by way of a bus. It gave me time to think and see different things. Days were going by fast, and I had no idea what type of job I would acquire. But whatever it was, I would work it until it fulfilled its purpose.

The next day me and Gabrielle were talking and she asked if she could see me after work. Of course I said yes.

"What were you doin' before you came?" I asked her.

"Washing clothes. I just put all of our stuff in the dryer."

We gave each other a hug, and me not being able to resist her, I started to plant kisses on her cheek and on her neck. In between her giggling, she said, "You always tryna get you some in."

"I gotta take advantage. I don't never know how long you gone be around."

"Don't be like that. I'm not goin' nowhere."

"We'll see." I trailed kisses from her face down to her breast.

"No, Brandon, what if somebody catch us?"

"There's nobody out here thinkin' about us, plus we haven't invested any time together since we first seen each other."

"I know, we just have to find the right time." Then out of nowhere, she said, "I shaved my pussy yesterday. Look." Then she pulled down her jogging pants to reveal herself to me.

I leaned over in the seat, looked into her eyes. "You did this for me?"

She replied seductively, "Maybe."

We started to kiss as my right hand made its way to her treasure box. Of course I wanted our first sexual experience to be more intimate, but I wasn't complaining and just allowed things to flow. At first when I felt her, she wasn't wet, but after I massaged her pussy a little bit and then inserted two of my fingers, I felt the moisture of her walls. I took my time as I caressed her pussy while we kissed. I wanted to make her cum, but with me being inexperienced sexually due to me being away so long, my confidence was not high.

"Ooh, baby."

"You gon' cum for me?"

In between her breathing heavy, she said, "Umm . . . Uh, I don't know."

I knew I couldn't perform how I wanted due to the way she was positioned, so I asked her to pull her seat all the way back.

"You won't be able to make me cum like this."

"I will if you let your seat back all the way. Plus, I want to taste you."

"Not today, Brandon. You gotta get back, and you can't miss your bus."

I initially resisted, but she was right. I was on a tight schedule and didn't really have a lot of room to maneuver at the moment. As I withdrew my fingers from inside her sweet walls, I brought my hand to my mouth to suck the juices off.

BEAUTIFUL CONSEQUENCES

"Don't do that," she said as she reached over and tried to grab my hand.

I pulled my hand away from her. "Why not?" And then I stuck both fingers in my mouth and tasted her juices.

"I shouldn't have done this. I don't know what I was thinking. I gotta stay away from you."

She drove me to the bus stop, we said our goodbyes, and as soon as I got out of her car, the bus was pulling up.

I called Gabrielle later and asked, "Why did you say you shouldn't have done what we did?"

"I shouldn't have, Brandon. I'm really vulnerable right now, so you can't be coming around tryna take advantage of me."

"Take advantage of you? Yeah right, if anything I'm the one being taken advantage of."

"Brandon, I'm for real, you know what I mean."

"Okay, Gabrielle, I hear you."

"Alright, enjoy the rest of your day."

"You too."

"You better tell me you love me."

"You know I love you."

She laughed. "You better. I love you too."

CHAPTER 48

After that experience, I was wanting Gabrielle now more than ever. It had been a few days since we spoke, and I had that feeling in my stomach that something was off. It was a kind of intuition I had developed since being involved with her. At times it was like I was dealing with two different people. One day she would be one way, and then out the blue she would switch and be the total opposite. I knew she was still involved with the guy she had been dealing with when she first turned on me. I would've expressed how I felt about what she was doing, but I knew I couldn't give her an ultimatum until I got a job, a place of my own, and a car.

My phone buzzed and I flipped it open. It was a message from Gabrielle. *Are you ok?*

I knew what was up, so I just replied and left it at that. *Yeah, I'm good.* Yet something in me wouldn't let it slide. *I told you when I came home I wasn't accepting you being with someone else. I'm not sharing you, you're mine. Whatever you got going on with him or anyone else is about to come to an end.*

My phone buzzed again. *I told you I have to figure things out, I have some of his stuff over here, I know I don't want to be with him but you have to let me work this out.*

I was getting tired of the excuses. I couldn't tell who

was in control, Gabrielle or the guy she was dating. A few days went by, and she started to call me again, so I figured the dude must not be around.

"So you think things are about to continue like how it was when I was in there?"

"What do you mean?"

"That you can come and go when you want to and put another man over me. The only other man you should be putting before me is your son, other than that we gon' have a problem."

"I know. It's just that I've been dealing with him off and on for like two years and the kids have gotten used to him. I know that's not what I want, but now you're here pressuring me. You know I don't like when you do that. I just want things to just be smooth with us so I can make the decision with a clear mind."

"Okay, Gabrielle. I'ma let you work through everything how you need to." We got off the phone and my mind went to what was at stake. I never wanted to put pressure on Gabrielle, but it just was my territorial possessive nature. There was no doubt that I wanted to marry Gabrielle and wanted her to carry and birth my first child. I knew what I wanted, yet it was all up to her, as always.

We continued to talk for the next few days, and she was expressing to me how she didn't have the rent money and it was due next week. For a long time, anytime she would mention any troubles she was having, especially financial, I would move without thought or question. But even though I was still moving, my mind was pondering why it was that she had just stopped talking to me for a while for this other guy, and yet didn't have money to pay the rent. It wasn't adding up for me, but that Saturday I went to the bank to withdraw a thousand dollars for her so she could handle what she needed to.

I messaged her, *I got that for you.*

A few minutes later, my phone buzzed. *What would I do without you?*

Don't go soft on me now, you would have figured it out.

No I'm serious, you're always here for me and always have my back and make sure me and the kids are ok.

I made a promise to you and I plan on keeping it.

She came to meet me on the side of town I was on and had her daughter Aaliyah with her. This was my first time actually meeting Gabrielle's daughter. I spoke to her, but she didn't say anything back. Gabrielle said it was because she was used to her ex, and I understood that. I handed her the envelope with the money in it. "Thank you so much. How did you get all this so fast?"

"You're asking a lot of questions. Don't worry about all that. If I say I got you, I got you."

"You always have my back. I love you for that. What are you about to do?"

"Probably just sit back and chill until I have to go back in."

"I'm about to go back to my sister's and get David and then go home. First I'ma take this money and put it in the bank. I get nervous with so much money on me."

We said our goodbyes and I continued with the rest of my evening. A few days passed, and while I was at work Gabrielle called me.

"I need to talk to you. Can I come see you when you get off?"

"Yeah."

Whatever it was, I could tell she was anxious to talk to me about it and get it off her mind because she was waiting outside for me as soon as I got off work.

"Hey."

"So let me tell you about William."

"Before you get into whatever it is you wanna talk about, do you know where a post office is around here? I have to mail something to my mom."

"Yeah, I do."

On the drive to the post office, she started talking about how she was on social media and saw how William's recent baby mommas were basically talking about their personal business in regards to William. Just typical angry talk about how they regretted their relationships with him. At the end of the day, I could care less, but I understood her perspective with feeling like she wasn't the only one who had issues with the father of her child. I went into the post office and mailed the package and got back into the car. One thing that I couldn't wrap my mind around was how people would just put all their personal business out on the internet for everybody to see. It was like whatever a person thought or felt, they would go right to make a comment or post about it, not even really thinking about the impulsive action they were making or how it could have a ripple effect later. I felt that social media was just another distraction for the people who didn't want to deal with or handle the real problems in their lives.

BEAUTIFUL CONSEQUENCES

I said, "At the end of the day, William is living life on his terms and it's nothing wrong with that. His decisions are his decisions and only he will inevitably have to accept the outcome of them all, just like the rest of us."

"That's true." Then there was a brief pause. "I know you probably don't want to hear it, but I need your thoughts about something. It has to do with my ex."

"Gabrielle, you know I don't wanna hear about nothing that gotta do wit you and somebody else. But since you wanna tell me so bad, go ahead."

"Okay, and thank you for being considerate. Anyway, I feel like he been playin' me this whole time. I knew he was still messing around wit his baby mom, and when I sent him some money not too long ago, she had the nerve to message me and said 'good looking for the money.' Then he texted me by mistake something that he meant to send to another woman and—"

"Not to cut you off, but first off, you been goin' back and forth wit this dude for like two years and every time I hear about 'um, it's always some negative shit. One day you like 'he did me like this and he did this to me' and the next day you right back wit 'um and leave me hangin' in the process. All this sound like some clown shit to me. You already know what it is and what he got going on, and you been goin' along wit it this long, so what the fuck you complainin' about it now for? This is why the two of you keep getting into it. You not playin' yo role. You got comfortable wit being a side bitch, and now you want main-bitch privileges, and the game don't go like that."

Gabrielle's eyes got big as she turned and briefly looked

at me. Then she put her eyes back on the road. I knew exactly what that look meant. That was the face of accuracy, the surprised look of *damn, you right*.

"You tryna switch shit up after you already been locked in this position for two years. You want more, but that's not what the arrangement was and that's why he can't give you that. He never had room for nothin' more than the role you been playing."

"Let me see yo dick."

What she said was definitely a curveball. I didn't even know what to think at first. It was more of a demand camouflaged as a question. "What?"

"You heard me. I said let me see yo dick."

"Nah, if you not gone eat it, you can't see it."

"Brandon, come on, you not gonna let me see it?"

Of course I was. I unbuckled my belt and pulled my pants down. She reached over and pulled my dick all the way out of my boxers and began massaging it while she drove with her other hand. She could make me hard as a rock with little or no effort. She was my burning desire, and nothing in life enflamed me the way she did. She continued to stroke my dick while she drove until I decided to bring things to a stop. I wasn't the one for being teased, plus my thirst for her wouldn't allow me to just accept her massaging me with her hand, so I gently removed her hand off my rock-hard dick and put it away. She pulled up at Steve's house, and I directed her to park in a reserved parking spot since we wouldn't be there for too long anyway. I still had a little time left before I had to be back at the halfway house, so we sat in the car for a little while.

BEAUTIFUL CONSEQUENCES

"So you just gone tease me like that?"

"What do you mean?"

"You got my dick hard, I told you that you couldn't see it unless you was gone eat it."

"No, Brandon, it's broad daylight outside, and what if somebody see us?"

"I don't see nobody out here right now, plus nobody that's out here is payin' us any attention." I pulled down my pants and she could see my hard dick extending, pushing the limits of my boxers. I put my hand over hers and gently brought her hand to feel it. I pulled it out of my boxers, and she started to stroke it. "Stop playin', Gabrielle, you wastin' time. I been locked up so long, I'm more than likely gone cum quick anyway."

"You definitely gon' nut." She leaned over into my seat with my dick in one hand, then she started to lick and lather it with spit. After she licked the length of my dick, she put it in her mouth and began to suck it. Just as I thought, after only a few strokes of her wet mouth on my dick, I felt that I was about to nut. I was pissed because I felt I wasn't even getting the chance to fully enjoy the experience I had waited years for, but at this moment there was nothing I could do. I held on as long as I could, and as I was about to get ready to release, I put my hand on the back of her head, and simultaneously as I did that, she rose up from her position.

"Damn, why you stop? You was supposed to keep going."

"That was quick." After she said it, she reached into her

center console to grab some wipes and handed them to me so I could clean myself off.

"I know. But you was supposed to keep going until I was hard again."

"You wanted me to swallow all that?"

It was almost time for me to be back to the halfway house, so I started to get my things together. We hugged and kissed passionately, but as I was getting out of the car, she said, "That dick better be clean."

I thought for a minute about what she was saying. "I don't have sex without a condom. That's something only reserved for you."

"But guys like to get their dick sucked without one."

I paused and thought for minute. "That's true, but I'm good."

"You about to hop and skip back to the place," she said laughing.

"Not really. I didn't even last long enough to even enjoy it. But I'll be alright until next time. I'll talk to you later."

"Okay. I love you."

"I love you too."

"You better."

CHAPTER 49

It was finally the time for me to obtain actual employment for a real wage. I had filled out numerous applications for jobs that I felt offered enough money to not only pay what would be my forthcoming list of bills but also give me the leverage to save money. I was given some information about a job fair that was taking place in West St. Paul and decided to attend. The very next week I got a call for an interview, and after that interview, they informed me that all I had to do was pass a drug test and I had the job. I was excited to be able to make some real money to start positioning myself to accomplish my financial goals.

"I got the warehouse job I told you about," I told Gabrielle.

"That's really good. I know you're feeling better about that."

"Yeah, now I can start to balance my life a little better."

"David asked about you."

"Oh yeah, what did he say?"

"He just was asking me where you were, so I'm guessing he wants to see you. What do you have goin' on today?"

"Nothing really."

"Well I have a few errands to run, so I'ma come get you and you can tag along with us."

"I don't have a problem wit dat." The last time I saw David, he couldn't even talk, all he would do is look and smile, but now he was eight going on nine. When I got into the car I spoke to David and Aaliyah, and they both said hi in a shy manner. I had to make a wire transfer, so I had Gabrielle take me to Walmart. The girls decided to wait in the car, and David went in with me. "So what's your favorite subject in school?"

"I like science."

"That's good, that's one of my favorite subjects too. Science has so many different levels to it. You never really can get bored with that. Your mom told me you play for Jimmy Lee basketball team. Do you like that?"

"Yeah, I really want to get good so I can play when I get older."

"As long as you practice and stay dedicated, you can do whatever you put your mind to."

As we were making our way through the store, David said, "You act like my dad." I couldn't do nothing but laugh at his comment. Once we got back to the car, I gave both of the kids twenty dollars, and I left to carry on with my day.

Next time I spoke to Gabrielle, I asked her, "What are you doin' for David's birthday this year?"

"He said he wanted to have a party, but I don't think I'ma do one this year. He said he wanted these Jordans that come out a few weeks before his day."

"I'll make sure he get 'um."

A few days went by, and I didn't hear nothing from Gabrielle, and I started to feel that familiar feeling in my stomach like something was wrong. I texted her a few times and got no reply. As I was out on a pass on Saturday, I got a text message from Gabrielle.

I hope all is well.

I instantly got upset. In my head, I was thinking, *What the fuck do you mean, you hope all is well?* I didn't want to respond aggressively, so I played it cool. *Gabrielle, what's wrong with you and why haven't I heard from you?*

I'm back with my man. I was furious that she was allowing an outside force to compromise our relationship. It was like she was throwing her relationship with this guy in my face on purpose, like she wanted to deliberately bring me pain.

Why are you back with him, when you know you want to be with me?

I don't want to be with you, I love him and I am going to work things out with the man I love.

I didn't know what else to say, so to save myself the heartache I asked her what David's shoe size was and let her know that before his birthday we could meet so she could get his shoes, after that we didn't have to talk anymore. She replied okay. I was lost in a dazed trance for a minute. I knew she was lying and didn't love that other guy, she loved me, but I couldn't figure what my next move should be. After I purchased David's shoes, I headed to the mall. I had to make another purchase to give to her when I gave her David's shoes. Once all the things I wanted to give her were in my possession, I went back to the halfway house. On my way back, the thought crossed my mind, *What am I doing? She doesn't love me, no matter what*

I do she keeps going in the other direction. Yet even with these thoughts running through my mind, my actions wouldn't waver from her. I was in love with her and I couldn't turn back until I had done all I could to win her heart. I was once again allowing my actions to show what it was I truly desired, and it was her. I could only wait and see what fruit would come from the seed I watered.

CHAPTER 50

It was my last week at my current position, and I would be starting my new job next week. My phone buzzed with a message from Gabrielle. *When can I pick up David's shoes?*

You can come and get them from my job tomorrow when I'm on my lunch break.

Riding the bus that morning with the bags I had, there was a lot on my mind, but I knew I had way too much on the line to get sidetracked by anything. I put everything in my locker and carried on with my day. When it was around that time, I received a text message saying that she was outside. After I got the bags out my locker I went outside and got in the car with her.

"What's in the bags?"

"David's shoes and something for you and Aaliyah."

"What is it?" As she reached in the back to see what was in the bags, I stopped her. "You can see once I leave."

"Thank you for his shoes. He really wanted them."

"No problem. I told you I would get 'um for him. I keep my word."

"I know. Why are you like that?"

"It's just me." My lunch break was ending, so I had to get back. "I gotta get back to work."

"Okay, love you."

I didn't respond. I just got out the car and went back in the building. As I got back to work, my phone buzzed. *Why would you do that?*

Even though I knew what she meant, I responded like I didn't know. *What do you mean?*

You know what I mean, never mind just call me when you get off bighead.

I carried on with my day as if everything was normal, and on my bus ride back, I called her.

"Hey."

"Hey." Things were quiet for a moment. "Why did you say 'why would you do that'?"

"Because, you know what I mean. All this stuff, I know what you doin'. You puttin' pressure on me."

When I had gone to the mall, I had made a trip to the Pandora store. I went in there looking for a new charm for Gabrielle's bracelet and to purchase a bracelet for Aaliyah as well. I took my time as I looked over all the different charms that would fit her bracelet. I didn't just want anything. I needed something that would speak to her and let her know I was serious. After contemplating two pieces, I settled on a nice size heart with crystals inside of it that had a keyhole in the middle of the heart with a key attached on the outside of it. To me it was perfect. That piece said everything that needed to be said without uttering a single word.

"Is there anything else I could possibly help you with?" a salesperson asked me.

"Actually, I was looking for another bracelet for the daughter of the woman that I chose the charm for."

"If you would like my opinion, I think you should maybe get her a necklace, since by her being younger she might not keep up with a charm bracelet."

"That sounds like a good idea. I think I'ma go with the necklace instead."

The last thing I needed to do was to find two matching charms. I decided on a charm for Aaliyah that said "daughter" that she could put on her necklace and a charm that said "mother" for Gabrielle to add to her bracelet.

Gabrielle said, "Why would you give me all this stuff? I can't believe you."

I had done all I could to fight for her love, and at this point I was done. Even after she told me she was going back with her ex, I still did all the things I said I would do before I was released from prison. But now I had to let her go her own way.

CHAPTER 51

It had been days since I talked to Gabrielle, and to my surprise, I had no urge to contact her and no negative feelings that she hadn't called me either. I was on a pass for a few hours at Steve's house and only had one hour left before I had to go back to the halfway house. As I was sitting on the couch thinking, Gabrielle called. I didn't answer. I really didn't feel like talking and really didn't have nothing to say. She called again, and even though I didn't want to talk to her, I answered. "What's up?"

"What are you doin'?"

"I'm thinkin'. What do you want, Gabrielle?"

"Why are you talkin' to me like that?"

"Gabrielle, I'm tired of wastin' my time wit you. You said you was back wit yo ex, so do dat and keep yo ass ova dat way. Why the fuck do you keep botherin' me? Leave me alone and just do you." I hung up.

I was beginning to develop a zero-tolerance perspective when it came to her antics. I would be able to understand if I was doing something wrong to her, but it was starting to perplex me as to why she was making loving her so hard. My phone rang again. "What?"

"Brandon, I'm sorry I . . . I just don't know what to do."

I could tell she was crying, but at this moment I could care less about her tears. "What the fuck do you mean, you don't know what to do? Continue on doin' what you said you was gone do. I'm cool wit us not being in each other's lives anymore."

"What! Brandon, no. I love you, and I can't have that. The kids need you. I need you. I don't want us to not be in each other's life. I love you."

"Gabrielle, I don't have time for this back-and-forth shit wit you. If you wanna be with somebody else, then go down knat path, but stop tryna pull me wit you because I'm not goin'. If you love these other dudes so much, then let them do all the heavy lifting and stop callin' me when you want some substantial shit done. Since you wanna impress them so much, let them support you, care for you, and love you. I'm cool on you."

"No, we are not doin' that. We are going to take things one day at a time and see where our relationship goes, but stop talkin' crazy. You not goin' nowhere and I'm not goin' nowhere and that's all there is to it."

"Whatever, Gabrielle. I gotta get back, so I'll talk to you later."

CHAPTER 52

Now me and Gabrielle were talking every day, and it seemed like nothing could keep us apart. I was at work and talking to her through my headphones, which made it hard for the supervisors to tell whether we were actually on the phone or listening to music. Yet nothing could have prepared me for what happened next.

"Brandon, I have to tell you something."

"Good or bad?"

"I did something bad."

"What did you do, Gabrielle?"

"I don't want to tell you."

"You have to."

She paused for a minute. "I got a tattoo."

"A tattoo of what?" My mind kicked in high gear. "I know you not tellin' me what I think you tellin' me."

"I got a tattoo of his name."

I paused, not to gather my thoughts but to attempt to neutralize what had shaken my whole universe. In that moment, no matter with all the energy I tried to muster up, I couldn't fight it. "I have to call you back."

I rushed to the bathroom. I went into the biggest stall, locked the door, and just allowed what was going to happen to happen. I couldn't hold back the tears. Even though I could not describe what I felt, I knew what it meant.

While I was away, I told her that no matter what she did, if one of three particular things were to occur, she would be leaving me no choice but to let her go. No rings, no tattoos, and no babies. Now she had committed two out of three offenses, which was starting to force me to believe that she did not care or respect or honor my word.

My phone buzzed with a message. *I'm so sorry, I only did it to make him happy and I regret the decision I made.*

I decided to call her back instead of texting her my response. "I want you to know I will always love you—"

Before I could continue, she asked, "Brandon, what are you about to do? Can you just tell me so I can know?"

In a calm voice, I said, "I just can't do this anymore."

"Brandon, no, I said I'm sorry. I don't even wanna be wit him. I know that is not the type of relationship I wanna be in. I'll get it covered up. You can't leave me, I'm not lettin' you go nowhere."

I couldn't believe what was happening. She actually had branded herself with another man's name. In my eyes she had to love him to put his name on her, even though she claimed she only did it to make him happy. I was starting to notice a pattern with her. It was like when her ex was around, Gabrielle would act like she was happy and he was the man for her. But then when he was gone and she would talk to me, it would be the complete opposite. I loved Gabrielle with all my heart, yet she was doing way too much, and I didn't know how we would move forward from this.

It was like no matter what I did she always chose to go in the opposite direction. She made loving her to be one of the most complicated things possible, when really to me it was all so simple. How would I look loving and catering to a woman with another man's name on her? I was struggling so hard with looking past and accepting her course of action for the sake of our relationship. I wanted to be with her more than anything, but this was pushing it to the limit.

CHAPTER 53

I was on my way to Gabrielle's house. This would be my first time being there since she moved, and of course I was excited, but I was also focused. Taking this ride to her house was a huge risk for me. Steve let me drive one of his cars, but all I had was a driver's permit, and I wouldn't be able to take my road test for another ninety days. Technically I was supposed to get permission from the halfway house to drive. If I was pulled over, not only could I lose my permit, but I could be sent back to prison for violating the rules. After I said a silent prayer, I put her address into the GPS in his car and got on the road. It had been a long time since I had drove a car, but I guess it was one of those things that, once you learned, you couldn't forget. I pulled up to the apartment complex and parked, then called Gabrielle.

As I sat downstairs waiting for her to let me in, I looked all around the complex. This was definitely a lot better than where she just moved from. No easy entry, the parking was a lot better, and the building was more upscale and comfortable looking.

Gabrielle opened the door. "So how was the drive? Did you find the place okay?"

"The drive from where I was actually was smooth, and it was a straight shot on 94 so that was cool."

"Yeah the freeway makes it smooth, but coming around the curve to get to my place is what throws people off sometimes."

As I followed behind her my thoughts began to race, but I did what I could to settle my mind.

"My mom took the kids with her, so it's only us for right now. Let me show you around. This is the kitchen. I like that the sink is a nice size and that the appliances are stainless steel. Do you like my color scheme for the living room?"

"Yeah, you put it together nice."

"At first I didn't know if it would work, but the green and blue came together well and then I found some really nice pillows that I added. This is the kids' room. I decided to get them bunk beds for now until we move again, and then they'll get their own rooms. They have their own bathroom." Looking at the kids' room, I couldn't do anything but smile seeing all the toys and different colors that made their space fit them and their personalities.

"This is my room. I decided to put lights around my curtains to give it a flair of character instead of it just being basic curtains." As I was looking around I was paying attention to all the different soaps and lotions she had. I wanted to know what all products that she liked.

"Oh, I forgot to show you the balcony off the living room." As I stepped out onto the balcony and looked over the parking lot, my thoughts drifted to how far things had come. Not too long ago I was locked away with no control over my life, and now things were slowly coming together.

"Brandon, you okay?"

"Yeah, why you ask me dat?"

"I don't know, just the look on your face. Come to my room with me while I do my hair. You can sit on my bed. This shouldn't take me too long."

Sitting there watching her in the mirror as she went through her process, I started to feel that I should address what we didn't have an understanding about. "Gabrielle, what's goin' on wit us?"

"What do you mean?"

"You know what I mean."

"Brandon, what do you want me to say?"

"I wanna know what we doin'. Are we moving forward together or what?"

She looked at me with those brown eyes that seemed to have me hypnotized, and then she looked away and said, "I need to take a shower." Then she got up from the chair and started to strip off her clothes.

I stepped over to her. "I'm not about to let you keep runnin' from this. We gon' finish this conversation."

"Brandon, I'm not runnin'. I need to take a shower."

My thoughts escaped my mouth before I could think about it. "I'm getting in wit you."

"Brandon, no you're not." She laughed and shook her head, then went into the bathroom and stepped into the shower, closing the curtain behind her. I immediately started to take off all my clothes until I was as naked as she was, then walked into the bathroom and pulled back the curtain as I stepped in.

"Brandon, what are you doin'? Get outta here."

"I told you I was takin' a shower wit you."

"I heard what you said and I told you that you couldn't. You're invading my personal space, Brandon. Get out."

The tone she was giving me made me feel she was serious, so I exited out the shower and back into her room. A few minutes later, she cut off the water, exited the shower, and grabbed a towel out of her closet to begin drying herself off. I started to make my way toward her. "Why you actin' like dat?" I asked her.

"What do you mean? It's just a lot, and oh my God you're naked! You need to put on some clothes."

"I don't know why you keep actin' like you don't love me."

"Because I don't love you like that. What don't you understand about that? Brandon, put on some clothes. You're makin' me uncomfortable."

I began to put all my clothes back on. My mind transitioned to what I needed to do next, so I went into my backpack and pulled out a few sheets of paper. As she saw me remove the paper from my backpack, she asked, "What is that, another love letter? Let me see it." But her voice was kind of insulting.

"It's not another love letter. It's something I wrote after you told me that you wasn't coming to come see me at the halfway house." After that, I had needed answers. I had gone into the chapel room we had in the unit so I would have some peace and quiet and written out a list of thirty-one questions that I needed answers to in order for us to bury our relationship and move on with our lives. I had known that even if Gabrielle didn't come see me when I was released, one day I would have an opportunity to find out from her what exactly our relationship was and meant to her. Now was the time.

"What is it then if it's not a love letter?"

"It's a list of questions that I want to know the answers to."

Gabrielle burst out in laughter. "That's that jail shit. Okay, well, ask me den."

Her tone and her words were shaking me up to the point that I couldn't think straight. My emotions began to cloud my thoughts, and with over thirty questions, I didn't see how I would be able to make it through the Q&A segment. There were a few significant questions that I had to have answers to now.

As Gabrielle stood combing her hair in the mirror, I stepped closer to her so I could look her in her eyes as I asked my question. "Has any other man in your life shown you the type of love I have?"

"No," she said fast, and then looked away from me.

"Then why are we not together?"

"Brandon, I just don't see you that way. It's a cold world out here, and the sooner you realize that, the sooner you'll get over this."

With my emotions all over the place I couldn't decipher what she was saying properly. I didn't know if she just said she was stringing me along the whole time or what. "I don't see what's so hard about us being together when you know you love me."

"Brandon, it's like your love is so deep and serious and it scares me. I've never had that before, and that's why I keep running away from you. And I don't want people talking bad about me because I decided to be with you. William and his family already don't accept my son and disrespect me, and if we're together it'll just make things worse. On top of that, my son knows you as his uncle, even if not by blood, that's what he thinks you are. I love you, Brandon. My own brother said he felt that you should have been my son's father. He looks at you as family. Look at you, we can't be around people and you actin' like this. They'll know we got something going on. I just don't want to confuse everybody with us being selfish with our actions."

I heard everything that she had to say, and always being the loving man I was toward her, I understood. But I was crushed. How were we going to be able to move forward now? With all that had transpired between us, what type of a relationship could we really have? I knew I would always want more than just a friendship with her, but that meant we would continue to clash and possibly destroy the connection we did have.

"I'm sorry if I messed up our relationship," I said. "I never meant to do dat. I've just never felt dis way before about anybody, and I love you."

She wrapped her arms around me and guided me to her bed and we sat down. She laid my head on her chest and started to rock back and forth with her arms around me. "I don't ever want you to think that I don't love you because I do. The relationship we have, no one can take that away from us, nobody. We both know what we mean to each other, you have always been there for me, and I will always be there for you. If the circumstances were different, there's no doubt in my mind that I would marry you and have your babies. I don't know what it is, but we just have always clicked from the very beginning and I don't want to lose that. It's going to be okay. We are going to get through this. You're my best friend." We sat there for a few minutes in silence and then she pushed me, and when my back hit her bed, she jumped on top of me and straddled me. "Now, I could just give you some of dis pussy, but then that would have things all crazy." Then she started rotating her hips and jumping up and down as if we were having sex.

"I wish you would. Maybe I wouldn't be so crazy over you. It would probably calm me down."

"I bet it would, you walking around here wit yo dick all out like you King Kong. You think I'm about to let you fuck me wit all dat? Nah, that's horse dick," she said in a slight laughing tone. I guess she seen that my mind was wondering. "Come on, Brandon, we gotta lighten up the mood in here. I don't want you down thinkin' too much about this. If we are meant to be then we will be, but don't let me get you off track. You're home now and I'm happy you're out."

Regardless of how I felt about our relationship status, she was right. I needed to focus my mind on other things. My mind started to drift back to a few conversations me and Mr. Washington had before I got released, how he'd told me that once I got back on my feet she'd come running to me.

Now my focus was starting to shift into proper perspective. I was still locked up really, even though I was in a halfway house. I didn't even have a car nor a place of my own, and for any man to be taken even a tad bit serious, he had to at least have those. At this point I decided to fall back from putting so much energy into us being into a committed relationship and transitioned my energy into building my foundation on solid ground. Once I got my affairs in order, then I could come back to the situation at hand.

CHAPTER 54

I began fixating my mind on the things that I knew would be building blocks for a solid foundation. Within a few months' time, I would need a place of my own and a reliable vehicle, one that could not only get me back and forth to work but that would be able to withstand the upcoming winter months. Also, I knew I needed a way to start building my credit. After opening a bank account, I was informed that I didn't have a credit score, which was better than having no credit. I invested in a secure card to start giving me some sort of credit background. I knew that without my credit being in good order, I wouldn't be able to make some of the power moves that I had on my agenda. Me and Gabrielle continued to talk regularly, not so much about us but everything that surrounded us, the kids, how I was adjusting to being out, and some of the things that bothered her in her life.

"I'm like, why should I have to walk away from the relationship with nothing, when I had everything coming into the relationship. It's like I lost myself in these past few years. I hate the fact that I allowed the kids to get close to him and get comfortable. He was helping me out financially, but it's been like he'll purposely put me in the hole, and I have to figure out how I'ma pay my rent and bills and I don't know why I keep putting myself in a fucked up position where I need somebody. He's in and out of town plus when he's mad, it's like fuck me and what I got going on. Even now it's Christmastime and I don't have any money to get the kids gifts. I start my new job but won't get paid until after Christmas and I feel like a horrible mother, plus all my credit cards are about to be due and I'm so frustrated with the position I put myself in. I don't wanna go back to being in a relationship wit him. I know it's toxic and he doesn't want the best for me, but I just don't have the money to take care of all that I need to right now."

I understood how hard things could be for any single person figuring out how to make it in life, let alone a woman with two children. Plus, I didn't want her to feel like she had to be in a relationship that she knew wasn't good for her, just because she needed some financial help at the moment.

"I want you to make a list of the major things the kids want for Christmas and what the dollar amount comes out to. After that let me know how much each of your credit cards are and the upcoming dates."

"Brandon, why do you want me to do all that? I mean—"

"Gabrielle, could you just do what I asked you to do please?"

"Okay."

With Christmas a few weeks away, I didn't want to wait until the last minute to get the kids what they wanted, so I asked her to meet me on an upcoming day when I would be out on a pass. We met in the parking lot of Walmart, since I had to go in there anyway to look for some work boots. She was already there waiting, and once I got there, I got in the car with her for a minute.

"Why did you have us meet here?"

"I'm about to go in here to see if they got the type of work boots that I need."

"Oh, okay." Then I handed her the envelope. "What's this?"

"That should take care of the things you sent me on the kids' Christmas list."

"Brandon, how much is this?"

"A thousand."

She just looked at me, then sat back in her seat and started shaking her head. "Brandon, where are you getting all this money from? Are you back out here in the streets again?"

"NO, you know I'm not on knat type a time. I just don't want the kids to not have at least some of the things they want for Christmas."

Things got quiet for a minute. "Thank you so much. You always make sure me and the kids are good. I'ma start going to get their stuff asap."

"Don't worry about it, I told you I got yo back no matter what. I'ma head into this store so I can find these boots. I'll just talk to you later."

"Okay then. I love you."

"I love you too."

Once she got the kids gifts, she sent me pictures of what she got. Then when it came time for each of her five credit cards that was due, I gave her the money to pay for each one. And since she was starting a new job and was low on cash, I gave her money to fill her gas tank so she could get back and forth to work so she wouldn't have to stress about that until she got her first check. I just wanted to take the pressure off of her so things wouldn't seem so overwhelming and to let her know that I loved her.

I knew what I wanted, and despite all the things that threatened to come in between us, I still wouldn't waver my attention from her. She was my desire, and I was willing to do whatever to please her and bring her comfort. One mandatory obligation that I had while staying in the halfway house was that I was forced to attend two "pro-social groups" per week in order to be able to leave on the weekends. They just wanted you to attend two classes that were based on self-improvement. Most of the residents went to AA classes or Drugs Anonymous classes, which gave them extra time to be out of the house, so I decided to attend a class for people supporting each other to stay clean from heroin addiction. The first few times I went it was only to get out of the house and get some fresh air, but one day I started to listen to the stories of struggle being told by the people attending the group. As I listened, I realized the similarity between myself and some of the speakers. The way they spoke about this specific drug is how I felt about Gabrielle. At that moment, I came to terms with the fact that I was addicted to her. Even with all the pain and signs letting me know that she wasn't good for me, I just couldn't seem to let her go. She was my angel and my devil.

I was on my way back from work and made sure to call her so I could hear her voice before going back in.

BEAUTIFUL CONSEQUENCES

"Hey."

I could tell that something was off with the tone in her voice. "What's wrong?"

"It's something wrong wit my car. It started this morning but now it won't start at all. After work my coworker waited with me until it started again, but once I got home and cut it off, it wouldn't start back up. Now I'm tryna figure out what I'ma do about getting back and forth to work."

"What do you think is wrong wit it?"

"I don't know, but I don't even have any money to figure it out."

I was quiet for a minute, thinking to see if there was anything I could do. "I won't have any money until next week when I get paid."

"It's okay, I'ma figure it out. You can call me tomorrow when you come out."

"Okay. I love you, and don't let that stress you out. We'll figure it out."

I hated to be in a position that I couldn't take action. I always felt that a man should provide for the woman he loved and do all things to make her feel secure, yet at this moment I couldn't assist her with what was going on. What good was I to her if when she needed someone there, I couldn't support her? We spoke briefly about her possibly getting a rental car so she could get back and forth to work and take care of her daily business, but I couldn't afford to cover the whole bill. The next day, we were on the phone brainstorming about the options she had, but I could tell she was unsure about what she should do.

"Brandon, I have to tell you something."

"Okay."

"You know I have to be straightforward and I can't hide nothing from you. I talked to my ex about what happened, and he said he would come out here and help me with the things I got going on."

This only added to my humiliation. For the woman that I was in love with to have to ask another man for help couldn't have made me feel any lesser. I paused for a moment and then responded, "I thought you didn't wanna be wit him."

"Brandon, I don't wanna be wit him, but what else am I supposed to do? You know I need a vehicle."

"I understand."

"I had to let you know what was goin' on."

"I appreciate that." There really wasn't nothing else to say at that point, plus I was getting close to my destination, so we ended our call.

No matter what I did, it was always easy for her to waver from me. I did all I could to support her since she claimed she wanted nothing to do with her ex, but as soon as one thing came up that I couldn't take care of immediately, she contacted him. I was fighting a losing battle. What was the point of all the things I had just done if she was only going to run back to her ex anyway? If I couldn't give her the things she needed, what weight would my words really have? Relationships today were not built on the foundation of loyalty, consistency, or understanding.

BEAUTIFUL CONSEQUENCES

Every element of almost all relationships was a variation of the question, "What can you do for me right now financially?" If you could appeal to a person's deep-rooted attachment to instant gratification, they would leave whoever they had to behind just to get what they wanted in that moment, no matter how loyal someone was to them. I had to evaluate what I was noticing in not only her behavior but life in general, then figure out if this was all this really worth it.

CHAPTER 55

I was out on a twelve-hour pass, and I decided to start my day at Steve's house. Steve was very supportive of my transition from prison back into society. He even gave me a key to his apartment in case of an emergency. We sat at the apartment for a while conversing about what was going on in each other's life. Steve was one of the only people I trusted. He offered me the soundest advice, the same that would come from a father or uncle or best friend, from someone that had genuine love for you no matter what and wanted the best for you. Today I needed to use Steve's car to take Gabrielle to drop her car off at the shop, and since he had two cars, he allowed me to take one. It was a twenty-minute drive from Steve's house to hers. I just focused on making sure I did the speed limit the entire way there and paying attention to all surrounding vehicles so that I could avoid any collisions. I had a safe trip and pulled up to Gabrielle's apartment with no problems. She had told me prior to coming to look for a space with a visitor's parking sign in front of it, which I found not too far from her apartment.

After a few minutes she came downstairs to let me in and lead the way to her apartment. Once inside, she took me to her dining room table so I could sit down. David came into the room. "What's up, man? Where you been at?" he said as he gave me a hug.

"I been working. How you liking school, and how you doing?"

"I'm doing good. School is okay, I just need to get better at math."

"I'ma see when I have some off days and I'll come help you sometimes so we can practice."

"Alright, bet." It was crazy hearing him speak and seeing his characteristics as he was starting to grow into a young person.

After I concluded my conversation with David, Gabrielle said, "Brandon, you can come into my room." She was laying on her bed on her phone, and stood there for a minute. She said, "Come sit down next to me. Why are you standin' up actin' weird?"

"I just don't like to come into someone's space and make myself at home."

"Well, make yourself at home. My mom will be here in a minute. She's about to take the kids skating. You haven't met my mom, huh?"

"I can't say for sure. If I did it was a long time ago."

"What have you been doin'?"

"Nothin' really, just studying and takin' my time with everything."

"I'm takin' some of the load off you, Brandon, by lettin' my ex come back around. You know I don't wanna be wit him. Nothing has changed about that."

"Yeah, I hear you."

"I'm serious, I want us to take things slow. I want to

make sure I'm making the right decision with a clear mind about us being together."

"Okay, Gabrielle, baby. I hear you." As we were talking, Aaliyah and David came into the room and began playing with Gabrielle. It turned into a family royal rumble, and as I sat back and watched, I thought to myself and felt in my core that this was what I wanted. The family dynamic with Gabrielle as my wife, along with me loving her two children as if they were mine, genuinely and equally.

After the royal rumble was over, Gabrielle's mom walked in. "Mom, this is my best friend, Brandon. Brandon, this is my mom." We greeted each other and she began to gather all the kids things for their trip. The kids put on their coats and shoes, then came to say goodbye to their mother and me. Once they walked out the door, Gabrielle locked it and then came back into the room.

"You want a shot?"

"What you got?"

"Some Patrón."

"Yeah, that's cool." Even though I wasn't supposed to be drinking because I hadn't given the halfway house my weekly urine sample, I couldn't decline the offer. She went to the cabinet and pulled out a bottle, and we both took a shot.

"I'm about to get into the shower." Gabrielle began to strip off all her clothes. I didn't know what it was about her taking all her clothes off in front of me, if she just was that comfortable with me or if she was doing it to tease me. But seeing her strip in front of me was like me watching my favorite movie. Once she was completely naked, she started to head to the shower. I caught her in midstride and grabbed her hand, not too hard but firm enough to let her know I wanted her attention. I looked her in the eyes as I pinned her against the wall, put my left hand on her hip, and leaned in to kiss her while I palmed her left ass cheek with my right hand. After our kiss, she started to walk away, and I smacked her right ass cheek as she got into the shower. We both knew what was about to happen next. My mind began to go into overdrive. For so many years, this is what I had imagined, an intimate engagement with the woman that had been in my dreams for so long. With the woman that owned the rights to my heart, the woman who controlled my emotions, the woman that had caused me to manifest the purest love I had ever known.

As she was drying herself off, I admired her body. She had everything that I wanted in a woman. She wasn't fat but wasn't skinny either. Her ass had the perfect cuff to it. It was like she was made for me. Nothing else in the world meant more to me than her and the bond we had—now it was time to solidify that connection. She approached me and then directed me to the bed. "You need to come outta these clothes." She assisted me with taking off my clothes until I only had on a T-shirt and my boxers.

I wanted to do what I could to please her. "Why don't you lay on yo back on na bed. Come on baby, I been waitin' for this."

She laid on her back with a pillow under her head and then spread her legs, revealing the most beautiful pussy ever created. I had literally experienced dreams of this moment while I was away, and now for it to be a reality was

BEAUTIFUL CONSEQUENCES

surreal. Honestly, I was intimidated. I didn't know how to eat pussy for real. I had only done it maybe twice. I knew that giving Gabrielle the pleasure that I wanted to give her would be damn near impossible. I got down on my knees, lifted her legs, and attempted to please her. I was all over the place. I really didn't know what to do, so I was licking where I thought I should.

She could tell that I was having a hard time. "You gotta lick and apply pressure to the clit, baby." After she said that, she spread her pussy lips and rubbed a particular area, indicating for me to lick there, but I could not fulfill the task. "You gotta learn how to flick yo tongue, baby. It's okay, you'll get better." I didn't want to stop, even though I knew I couldn't please her. "Put it inside me, Brandon. I want to feel you inside me." She said it in a light voice but still, it was a demanding tone.

I got up off my knees, lifted her left leg, and inserted my hard dick inside of her. After all these years, from the connection we had before I went to prison, for our bond to only grow stronger while I was away for almost a decade, to now the undeniable love being expressed between us. For being gone so long without being able to have sex, I knew this would be a challenge. Almost right after I entered her walls of honey, I knew I was going to cum fast. In my mind, there was no point in climaxing fast with slow strokes, so I gave her the hardest, deepest strokes I could as I came inside of her.

As I was releasing the last of my semen, her voice came through my ear. "Why you haven't cum yet, who you been fuckin'?" When I didn't respond, she shifted her head so we were face to face. "Did you cum already?"

"Yeah."

There was a brief pause. "Have you had sex with anyone else?"

I was thrown off guard by the question. "What?"

"You heard me, I said have you had sex with anyone else?"

Throughout our whole relationship, I had never lied to her about anything, and even though I wanted to lie to her, I couldn't.

"Yeah."

ABOUT THE AUTHOR

Antwon Ri'Chard is a writer who lives in Minneapolis. *Beautiful Consequences* is his first book.

Made in the USA
Monee, IL
13 February 2024